35

SO-CRO-246

WITHDRAWN

67

Star of Randevi

Other Books by Marjorie McEvoy

THE SLEEPING TIGER
CALABRIAN SUMMER
ECHOES FROM THE PAST
THE QUEEN OF SPADES
EAGLESCLIFFE
WHO WALKS BY MOONLIGHT
THE WHITE CASTELLO
THE GRENFELL LEGACY
SOFTLY TREADS DANGER
NO CASTLE OF DREAMS

Marjorie McEvoy

STAR
OF
RANDEVI

DOUBLEDAY & COMPANY, INC.
GARDEN CITY, NEW YORK

1984

Library of Congress Cataloging in Publication Data

McEvoy, Majorie.
Star of Randevi.
(Starlight Romances)
I. Title. II. Series.
PR6063.A196S8 1984   823′.914
ISBN 0-385-19081-6

Library of Congress Catalog Card Number 83–16361

First Edition

For Therese Claire

Star of Randevi

CHAPTER ONE

Rakhee the dancing girl, posturing and pirouetting, sidled from the dais and moved slowly toward them, expressive hands working full-time.

Andhra eyed her closely. Oh, she was lovely, with all the attributes of youth and a pampered life. Plus, of course, skillfully applied paint and powder, flashing jewels and exotic silken draperies.

And so alluring, with all the wiles of the East behind her inscrutable eyes—eyes that could flash fire on occasion, or assume a doelike demureness and an innocence, if she so willed, that was patently a mask.

She willed it now as she paused a mere yard or two in front of Andhra and Prince Ranjana.

Rakhee's whole attention was on the prince. Obviously she was out to charm him and cared little for Andhra or any of the other spectators.

Andhra cast a quick glance at her husband. He was certainly not unresponsive to the pronounced assets of this delectable creature—the rounded breasts straining against the tight silk tunic, bound beneath by jeweled braid; the curvaceous hips and firm bottom, accentuated by the way her flimsy draperies were caught around the sensuous body with ribbons and laces; the painted, languorous eyes; and the flashing jewel clipped to one flaring nostril.

Loyal and loving husband notwithstanding, he was above all a splendid, virile specimen of a man, with a normal man's desires. And with their baby's birth imminent, it had been a long time since he had come to her and shared her bed through the long, sultry night.

Too long. It was providential that tomorrow they were leaving Cochpur Palace to take up residence in their own new home, the Summer Palace, up in the hills near beautiful Lake Komin.

How Andhra longed for that moment. The past month here in this vast and crumbling abode of Ranjana's uncle, waiting for the Summer Palace to be renovated to their requirements, had been trying in the extreme. Spite and intrigue were rife in the women's quarters where she had mostly spent her days, and indeed throughout the palace. It was clear to her that in spite of Uncle Balbir's unctuous overtures, he was at heart deeply mortified that the Summer Palace and the valuable estate of land and lake that went with it had been left to his nephew Ranjana and not to himself by his deceased elder brother. True, he himself already possessed this larger Cochpur Palace on the outskirts of the city, but without land to bring in some much needed revenue, the place was crumbling for want of repair. Balbir's personal income was sufficient only for his lavish style of living, with hunting parties and banquets and concubines acquired to offset the lost charms of his middle-aged barren wife, Madhumita.

Yes, he was a man to be feared and watched, Andhra felt instinctively. Still lean and hale in spite of his fifty years, the way he glanced at her with ill-concealed lust when he chanced on her alone made her squirm down to her bare feet. He had clearly made a favorite of this dancing girl, who came frequently to the palace to titillate his jaded palate. He was even now glowering at her from across the room for flaunting herself in front of Ranjana, his superior in every way. Perhaps he would give her a taste of his whip later, to teach her who was master.

It was a relief when the evening ended and Andhra could kiss Ranjana a chaste good night outside the women's quarters, and seek the sanctuary of her own austere apartment, attended only by Mumtaz.

Already she loved Mumtaz, the young Tamil chosen as ayah for the coming child. Mumtaz was patient, cheerful and wise beyond her twenty-six years. She would make a good and devoted nurse to the baby, and help smooth Andhra's own path through the first months in her new home. For with her largely

English upbringing, Andhra was somewhat unsure of herself as chatelaine of a palace, with many servants at her command.

"Peace, my princess. Thy time is at hand, and then again wilt thou be as slim as the willow tree and as beautiful as the dawn over the Nilgiri Hills. Then can you laugh at the garish wiles of Rakhee the dancer, for thy prince will have eyes for no one save his fair princess, the mother of his son," Mumtaz said soothingly.

Andhra smiled as Mumtaz drew off her sari, settled her among cushions and proceeded to take down and brush her mistress's lustrous black hair before braiding it neatly for the night.

Seated cross-legged on the floor behind her, Mumtaz hummed a soothing little tune as she deftly worked. Andhra felt vexation slipping away. This girl would turn out a treasure, like the old ayah who had cared for her and her adoptive sister Jenny, in the dear dead days before the Indian Mutiny scythed through the land, changing everything.

How far off that seemed, and yet it was only a few brief years. The past was over, but it had left its mark. Some, like Ranjana, had sifted out the best that the East India Company had left behind and were resolved to carry on the good work of improving the lot of the common people and the country as a whole, working harmoniously with the representatives of Queen Victoria, far away in London.

She and Ranjana had great plans. He was eager to extend and improve the estate that fate had thrown his way, thus giving work to more of the Tamil people, while Andhra had visions of founding a small hospital and school for the exclusive use of the estate workers and their families here in this remote southern town of Cochpur. It was greatly needed. So many of the children died at birth or before the first year. Too many of the workers had lives cut short by snakebite, typhoid, cholera and all the other tropical scourges, with no skilled help near at hand.

On these thoughts Andhra found herself settled among the cushions for the night, the faithful Mumtaz stretched out at her feet, ready to minister to her slightest whim. At their best Indian servants were marvelous, she reflected, smiling. They knew everything that went on almost before it happened. There was no real privacy. At times the lack of it exasperated her, brought up in the more formal atmosphere of Victorian England as she had been, yet it had its compensations.

She slept well and awakened early. Today was the beginning of a new life for herself and Ranjana—their first home, in which their child would be born; so many momentous happenings. Before then she must pay a visit to the towering Hindu temple nearby, with its intricate stone carvings and the benign statue of Nandi, the bull, Shiva's symbol. She would make an offering and ring the temple bell to ask for a blessing on the new life opening before her, and especially to pray for a son. Ranjana, like all Indian fathers, desired a son. It would be unthinkable to disappoint him. With the logic she had learned in England, she knew quite well that it would make no difference. The die was cast. The sex of her child had been determined even at the moment of its conception, almost nine months ago. Yet the mystic superstition that was the legacy of her Indian ancestors drew her to the temple like a magnet.

"This morning we go to the temple," she told Mumtaz. "Weave a wreath of fresh jasmine and marigold flowers, and bring rice and ghee. I've a fancy to make a last plea."

Mumtaz nodded her dark head. "That is good, my princess," and off she sped on her bare feet.

"Do you wish me to ask for a palanquin to be ordered?" she asked when she returned with the wreath of sweet-smelling orange and white flowers.

"No. The temple is not far. We shall walk. I don't care to ask favors in this household."

Andhra drew in great breaths of fresh air when they stepped outside into the faint mist of early morning, through which the sun already shone dimly. Even in the winter months, early morning and evening were the only comparatively cool hours of the day down in this southern tip of India.

They skirted the city, which was already bustling with life. Ox carts creaked their slow way, piled high with coir, the coconut-husk fiber that made ropes and matting; water buffaloes were being driven out to the rice paddies; gharries and rickshaws were being pulled along by sweating coolies; ele-

phants were setting out for work; and people were everywhere, scurrying along like ants before the sun triumphed and
slowed their pace to a measured crawl.

Walking gracefully in the leather sandals she always wore
outdoors because of the unclean paths, Andhra was a picture of
serene beauty. The shimmering purple silk of her sari hid the
thickened line of her figure beneath its loose folds, as the gossa-
mer head scarf draped over her shining black hair and held
across her mouth hid her lovely honey-colored face from the
gaze of all and sundry.

A pace or two behind as befitted her station, Mumtaz pattered in her bare feet, carrying the fragrant wreath and other
offerings. Passing Tamil women walking tall and straight, their
brass water pots balanced on their heads, glanced curiously for
a moment at this exalted member of their sex, then passed on
without envy. The gods decreed one's caste and station in life,
and nothing at all could change that.

Now from behind a cluster of graceful palms rose the great
gopura, the towering ornamental gates of the temple, fantastic
under its myriad stone carvings of gods, goddesses and mythi-
cal demons. Seven pillared openings rose heavenward like
ladders leading to celestial regions, topped by golden spikes
that caught the early rays of the sun and flashed fire.

Andhra paused in admiration. She could have spent hours in
contemplation of these stupendous achievements depicting
myths and legends that went back through the mists of time.
But her own time was limited. She must be back before breakfast if comments were not to be made.

Approaching the steps that led through the entrance, she
kicked off her sandals and climbed up.

A huge black image of Nandi the bull confronted her, serenely seated under his canopy. His almost benevolent expression brought a smile as Andhra motioned to Mumtaz to climb
up and throw the fragrant wreath around his neck.

Then she passed on to the inner temples, with their many
pillars and carvings, until she came to a small image of Shiva
seated on his sacred bull. Here she paused, murmuring her
plea for a son, before placing her offerings at his feet.

Now it was time to return, but on the way back Andhra

lingered for a moment at a much smaller temple that stood inconspicuously at the corner of a street. This was a living, breathing shrine, full of life and sound and the scent of incense floating strongly out. She placed an offering in a small bowl on a pedestal, then pulled on the bell rope, again voicing her desire for a son. The answering silvery jangle of the bell assured her that her wish would be granted.

After breakfast came the bustle of departure.

Andhra would have liked to ride side by side with Ranjana, who was seated commandingly on his magnificent horse Rajah, but her exalted status and her condition decreed that she travel in a palanquin, seated on soft cushions and carried by two bearers. Mumtaz followed in a less ornate doolie, with her mistress's clothes stacked around her.

From the crumbling palace in Cochpur to the Summer Palace was a six-mile ride up a gently sloping earthen track that was full of interest, with its wayside villages, terraced rice paddies, banana plantations and coconut groves. The villagers in their thatched huts made a precarious living, processing the coir and harvesting two crops of rice a year, except when the monsoon failed and famine stalked the land. This year the rains had been plentiful and all was well. It was the beginning of winter, the most pleasant time of year, when even at midday the sun's rays were not a fiery furnace to be shunned and the temperature reached a bearable eighty degrees.

"How are you faring, my pearl?"

Ranjana had paused beside her. Andhra's heart swelled with pride and love as she glanced up at him from between the curtains. How devastatingly handsome he was.

"All is well. In fact, I'm enjoying the changing scenes. Where does your estate start, my prince?"

"*Our* estate. We are just entering it, and I'm not impressed. It looks to have been neglected for a long time, which will make it easier for me to put my plan into action."

He had the future all mapped out. Burning with zeal to help his people and his country, he had been advised that tea was a better prospect for hill land than coffee or the more familiar crops that did poorly up here. He was all set to plow and clean as many of these neglected acres as possible and give the peasants a more secure life, with regular work and wages.

"I wonder how they'll take to the sweeping changes, and especially to tea plantations here," Andhra said shrewdly. "It's a new crop for them, and you know how suspicious they are of changes."

"It's been tried in Ceylon with considerable success. China and Darjeeling no longer hold the monopoly in tea, my love. They are too expensive for the mass market. This new strain can be grown much more cheaply down in these southern latitudes. Surely the peasants will accept change when they see it is to their advantage—new homes, regular work, better conditions for them and their children."

Andhra hoped he was right. They certainly looked wretched enough at present, the small children stark naked, the adults thin and ragged. Scrawny fowls and skinny, grunting piglets foraged in and out of the one-room shacks. Women sat pounding maize and millet, chanting a monotonous song as they worked, or thrashing clothes on stones by rivers, blessedly full after the rain. Nimble youths shinnied up the tall coconut palms to dislodge the brown nuts that gave them drink, food and many other things, or plowed small plots with primitive wooden plows.

Sanitation was nonexistent and water supplies were scarce and contaminated. Small wonder that disease was rife. Ranjana, with his Oxford education, thirsted to set his improvements in motion, but would these people understand and accept as he believed? He was from a northern branch of the family, a stranger to these coolies. Andhra prayed that they would take to him and his well-meant schemes with as much fervor as he himself possessed.

Before she had time to grow weary of the jerky movement over an unmade track, they had arrived.

Home. Dismounting, Ranjana drew wide the curtains of the palanquin so that she could admire the delightful vista open before her.

The Summer Palace, like so many hot-weather homes of the rulers, was built on an island in a small lake. Actually it was not quite an island, because a strip of land just broad enough for an ox cart to cross joined it to the mainland in the form of a graceful bridge, which enhanced rather than diminished the aloof charm of the building.

Andhra gasped in wordless admiration. It was truly enchanting, rising like a mirage from the blue lake, a picture in white marble and granite. Smaller than the Cochpur Palace they had recently left, it was infinitely more beautiful, a dwelling to thrill any woman, and now she was to be mistress here.

Ranjana smiled. "I knew you'd like it. I loved coming here as a boy to stay with my uncle, who, having lost both wife and family to malaria, was a lonely man. In later years he was ailing and crotchety, wanting no one around him. I almost forgot this delectable spot in the terrible events of the mutiny, assuming that he would leave it to his younger brother Balbir, but apparently he fell out with him and his barren wife and remembered the eager boy who used to amuse him. He must have decided I would make a better master here than Balbir, and by heaven, the estate looks as though it needs a firm hand."

"Somebody must have been in charge if your uncle was confined to the palace by ill health."

"Oh, there's a manager of sorts, I understand, but I can just imagine how he's been squeezing as much rent and taxes as he could from the wretched smallholders and lining his own pockets. He's certainly put little back into the estate, by the look of it. It's providential that changing over to tea will enable me to get rid of him honorably, since presumably he knows nothing of such matters."

Andhra thought of the new manager, who would be traveling down from Darjeeling with her adoptive sister Jenny in a few days' time. Robert Pearson had been helping to run tea plantations for many years and now welcomed the chance of managing a virgin estate. He was a man of excellent character and proven ability, Jenny had assured them, so Ranjana felt certain that he would prove to be the right man for the job.

Ranjana motioned to the bearers to pick up the palanquin and carry his bride across the bridge to her first home. Andhra caught a glimpse of the servants waiting in a body outside the palace and quailed. How thankful she was to have one loved and trusted attendant, Mumtaz, to smooth her path until she slipped more easily into this new and exalted life.

The plantation manager had pushed his way forward to greet them first as Andhra stepped from her carriage behind her husband. Hands folded before his face in the accepted manner of welcome or farewell, he glanced appraisingly at them. *"Namaste,* Your Highnesses."

"Namaste." Even as she returned the greeting, Andhra knew that she neither liked nor trusted this man. His eyes were sly, and his mouth was small and mean. He would surely not take kindly to being either dismissed or demoted to an inferior position.

But that was more Ranjana's problem than hers, she reflected as she bent her graceful head to receive the welcoming garland of marigolds the manager placed around her neck. She herself would no doubt have enough of her own in the form of servants grown slack and careless while their elderly master lay sick and impotent.

The manager's name was Shukur Thayar, she gathered as he moved aside to disclose the rest of the servants, a retinue of formidable proportions: bearers in striking blue livery with red cummerbunds and white turbans, the cook and his boys, the water carrier, the *dhobi wallah,* the *punkah wallahs,* the sweeper and the gardeners, plus several others.

Confronting this concentrated stare of curiosity, Andhra felt a touch of bewilderment until Ranjana reassured her in a murmured aside. "Don't worry. You'll mainly be dealing with the cook. He's the highest paid and the most important member of a household of servants. He practically runs the place from high to low."

He was quite right, Andhra recalled from the days leading up to the mutiny, when she had run her adoptive father's bungalow. The cook discussed menus with the memsahib, went to market and bought provisions with the money given to him, and squeezed as much profit for himself out of it as he could get away with. In her new exalted station as a princess, Andhra could have passed these duties over to others had she so wished, but she and Ranjana had both decided they would never be mere figureheads, living a lotus-eater life of pleasure like Uncle Balbir, but would take an active part in both estate and household and make the most of this gift so providentially flung their way.

The cook stepped forward now, hands humbly folded before his face, volunteering that his name was Gulam and that he vowed to serve them faithfully for the rest of his days.

In spite of these high-flown words, Andhra did not feel drawn to him. The face beneath the white turban was like a closed book, showing no sign of feeling or humility. Did he resent the appearance of a new master and mistress after a period of doing pretty much as he pleased since the death of his old master?

It was more than likely, and with the realization came a touch of misgiving. Suddenly this beautiful palace that was now her home seemed to pose a threat. A hint of menace lurked in the dim, shuttered rooms behind this sea of faces, bringing a conviction that things would not run as smoothly as she and Ranjana had confidently expected.

There would be tensions, conflict and perhaps even danger, she felt instinctively as she stepped through the arched gateway into the great courtyard, where a fountain tinkled musically and the rich colors of bougainvillea flaunted themselves like a rainbow over the gleaming white walls.

CHAPTER TWO

Andhra raised her arm and thrilled to the way the precious stones in her new bangle caught the light and flashed fire. It was Ranjana's gift to her for giving him a son. It must have cost a great many rupees—more than he ought to have spent, with all his plans for expansion and improvement of the estate, but all the more precious because it was given with all his heart.

Even more precious was the scrap of humanity cradled in his cot, draped in satins and laces. Little Sanjay was a perfect jewel, with his golden skin and raven hair and great brown eyes that looked out on the world in wonder during the brief times he was not sleeping. Already after only a few days Mumtaz adored him and would have sat crooning by his cot all day had Andhra not sent her about her business.

And today there would be another pleasure. Dear Jenny, with whom she and Ranjana had stayed after their marriage until coming down to the south, was arriving in the late afternoon on an extended visit.

What a contrast this would be to Jenny's bungalow in faroff Darjeeling. Compact and homely, the bungalow suited British-born Jenny and her engineer husband Mark Copeland perfectly, with its Victorian furnishings and cozy atmosphere, set in its hill-station position in the foothills of the Himalayas. In contrast, temperatures on the middle slopes of these Western Ghats on which the Summer Palace was built never fell very low, so the marble floors and airy courts made perfect living quarters for the environment.

Jenny would be both impressed and delighted, Andhra reflected, summoning up in her mind's eye the vision that would first greet her adoptive sister—the stunning white facade rising wraithlike from the deep blue waters of the lake, the majestic entrance doorway flanked by pillars, the soaring cupola rising above it, so typically Indian. The gardens outside were equally beautiful, drenched in color from shrubs and flowers revived by the recent monsoon and watered daily by the garden boys.

Neither could any fault be found inside in the suite of rooms Andhra and Ranjana had renovated for themselves. With their westernized outlook, they had installed a drawing room with comfortable chairs and modern furniture, a homely little dining room, several bedrooms and a bathroom with a couple of large hip baths, and tin mugs with which to douse themselves.

She had a notion that the servants did not approve. Changes went against the grain. The rambling, ornate rooms loaded with pictures, draperies and intricate carvings in ivory, sandalwood and teak that made up the rest of the place were more to their taste.

It mattered little. What did matter was the vague atmosphere of suspicion that pervaded the Summer Palace. In spite of her efforts to win favor, neither she nor Ranjana had been fully accepted here, and that was galling for two people who had only the welfare of the estate and its workers at heart.

Secretly Andhra suspected that Ranjana's Uncle Balbir was behind it. He had no doubt sown seeds of dissension before she and Ranjana had traveled down from Darjeeling, alleging that they were not the rightful rulers and with their westernized outlook would turn the old traditions upside down. He had no doubt made much of the fact that she, orphaned in babyhood, had been adopted by a British officer and his wife and brought up with their own daughter in British ways and outlook, while Ranjana, having been educated at an English university, would be equally unsympathetic to Indian customs.

Nothing was more likely to raise hostility among the palace servants and the estate coolies. Balbir, deeply resentful that he and his concubine son Satish had been passed over, was like a dog in the manger. If he could not have the Summer Palace and its land himself, he would do his worst to see that no one else enjoyed it.

There was a knock on the door, and Ranjana entered. He

gazed fondly at his sleeping son, then moved to Andhra's side. "How is my love this morning?"

Her answer was muffled by his lips seeking hers. Her heart beat faster. How devastatingly handsome he was, how hard and virile the arms that enfolded her, making her long for the time when he could share her bed again and they would know ecstasy together.

That would be another month yet. Custom decreed that she keep apart until the ritual cleansing ceremony in the temple, followed by public rejoicing, freed her for normal life again. Until then she must keep to the palace and its grounds, so Jenny was coming to keep her company and see the new heir. That was some compensation.

Ranjana's gusty sigh proved that he felt the same way. To distract him, she asked how things were going on the estate.

He shrugged. "Not entirely smoothly. The coolies don't seem too happy at the prospect of leaving their wretched little plots and huts and earning regular wages. The process of clearing land has been started, and the building of new homes, but tea as a crop is new on this estate, and you know their reactions to anything new."

"I can guess. Even so, I'm sure they'd have been less hostile to the prospect had they been left alone. I can imagine the sort of poison Balbir has been sowing among them, old vulture that he is. He'll never forgive you for inheriting the Summer Palace and estate from under his nose and against all his expectations, and his son Satish is just as furious, under his sly manner."

Ranjana nodded somberly. "It's an unfortunate start to all our plans. I'm glad Robert Pearson is arriving today with Jenny. Knowing all about tea growing, he may be able to convince them better than I that these innovations will ultimately bring prosperity to them and the estate alike."

Andhra had her doubts. Robert Pearson was English, like Jenny and her husband Mark. Although the mutiny was over, it was not yet forgotten. Queen Victoria, in faroff Britain, ruled India in place of the East India Company and had deprived many of the maharajas of much of their power. Otherwise things went on in much the same way—apart from a few like Ranjana and herself, who had learned a great deal from the

British and strove to incorporate the best of both worlds into the new regime.

Sanjay began to stir and whimper in his satin-lined nest.

"Feeding time and he knows it," Andhra said with an indulgent smile.

"Then I'll go. I've much to do. I'll see you at dinner tonight?"

"Of course. It's time I took up the domestic reins, with Jenny coming, not to mention Robert Pearson."

He kissed her lingeringly, his hands caressing the firm breasts that gave sustenance to his son. It was a wrench to push him gently away, because she so wanted him to stay.

Sanjay's voice was more demanding now. It reached Mumtaz, lurking outside, who darted in as soon as Ranjana left the room.

"The *chota sahib* is hungry. Come to Ayah then, my princeling," she crooned, picking him up.

"Unless I keep a firm hand, I can see he's going to be thoroughly spoiled," Andhra said, taking her son in her arms. But her tone was indulgent. She dimly remembered the warm relationship that had existed between her own ayah and herself in those long-ago days in northern India when a British garrison town had been her home, along with a modest bungalow, before she had been sent to school in England.

Now she had this magnificent palace, a prince for a husband, and a baby son. The gods had indeed showered blessings upon her; yet still there was a cloud on the horizon. They could only hope that it would gradually disperse when the estate people realized the new owners had only their good at heart.

Later that day Andhra stood surveying herself in the long mirror in her bedroom, an incredulous smile on her face. How marvelous it was to be again as slender as a swaying palm tree, and even more beautiful than she had been before Sanjay's birth. For now there was a sweet and tender expression of maturity on her lovely face that made it well nigh irresistible to any full-blooded male who happened to pass her way.

The green, diaphanous sari embroidered in lavish gold that now hung in classic folds about her was infinitely becoming.

How proud Ranjana would feel when he saw her, and how desirous of exploring her perfect, golden body again.

"A true princess," Mumtaz enthused, tugging at a fold of material here and tucking in an end there. "The prince and your guests will be dazzled as by the midday sun, but you must take care not to tire yourself. Remember, this is your first time up."

"What of it! I feel on top of the world." Andhra raised slender golden arms and spun around on her gleaming sandals until her draperies whirled and she looked like an animated flower.

There came a tap on the door, and Ranjana entered.

"Come and greet your guests, my pearl. They are even now crossing the bridge." He broke off, obviously spellbound.

"Don't upset the sari Mumtaz has arranged with such pains," Andhra warned as he caught her to him, but the warmth of her eyes belied her admonition, and it was only the need to hurry down to the courtyard that saved her from a bear hug.

They had only just arrived there when the guests were shown in.

"Jenny, how lovely to see you again!" Disregarding the warning she had just given Ranjana, Andhra enveloped her adoptive sister in loving arms and was hugged in return. "How well you look!"

"You, too, Andhra darling. Every inch a princess. I declare you grow more lovely every time I see you." Jenny stood back the better to admire this delectable Indian girl with whom she had shared all her childhood and teens.

"A perfect mistress for this magnificent home," she declared. "Such a contrast to me, a plain little memsahib in a homely little bungalow, with not even a child to boast about. You've beaten me there, too, but you deserve every bit of it. I'm sure I should never have survived those shattering episodes of the mutiny but for you."

"That's all in the past and best forgotten." Andhra's glance was on the man who had escorted her sister down from Darjeeling. He stood near Ranjana, waiting to congratulate her on the birth of her son. She had met him a few times while she was residing with Jenny, but had forgotten how rugged he was, and what an impact his corn-colored thatch of hair and steel-blue eyes made on a woman in this land of raven locks.

"Why Mr. Pearson, how nice to see you again. I hope the journey wasn't too tedious for you both."

"On the contrary." He grasped the hand she held out to him and smiled down at her. "And now that we've arrived, the splendor of the palace would justify a journey twice as long. Congratulations on it, your son, and this vast estate. I'm sure you'll reign over all with great charm."

"Only with the help of the most marvelous husband in the world," Andhra said hastily to dispel the fleeting frown on Ranjana's brow. Surely he couldn't be feeling a twinge of jealousy. That would be quite absurd.

After the visitors had freshened up and Jenny had taken her first peep at young Sanjay, they strolled in the beautiful grounds until dinnertime.

"A picture," was Robert Pearson's verdict, "but of course I'm even more eager to see and appraise the estate. The packages of seeds I've brought with me will keep, but the carefully packed cuttings will need planting as soon as possible."

Ranjana nodded. "I'm equally burning to make a start. Already I've had a few acres cleared. Virgin land with quite good soil. It's on the upper slopes of the estate, above the plots worked by the families that have settled here."

"What are they growing now?"

"Cinchona, cinnamon, pepper and other spices, but chiefly coffee. Spices on such a small scale are not very profitable, and lately the blight of *Hemileia vastatrix* has destroyed many of their *Coffea arabica* shrubs, so they're wretchedly poor. In consequence, they ought to be thankful that a ruler with progressive ideas has inherited the estate to help them, but I'm afraid that's not the case."

"The usual traditional prejudice against change, I suppose? Well, we'll just have to overcome it, kindly but firmly."

"You had better realize just what you're up against," Andhra said, and went on to explain about Uncle Balbir and his festering jealousy.

Robert Pearson shrugged. "One grows used to opposition in India. I guess we can overcome it if the land belongs to you."

Ranjana nodded. "Undoubtedly. The families have been paying a small amount in rent and taxes, that is, when the crops were flourishing. I suspect the present manager, Shukur Thayar, has been very much on the fiddle. Naturally he's going to feel very aggrieved at being deposed. Another thorn in our flesh, I fear. We'll have to decide what to do with him."

Both he and the estate would have to wait until morning, for now the brief twilight was falling, and it was time to go in to dinner.

Andhra enjoyed her first meal up. Gulam was an excellent cook, though she would have to be firm with him and show that she was no ignorant memsahib and would tolerate only a reasonable amount of fiddling with the market accounts. Imrat the house bearer, was also a credit to the palace as he waited at table in his immaculate blue coat and red cummerbund, although there was something about him that made Andhra unable to trust him completely. From the ceiling above hung the punkahs, pulled by ropes from outside the room and giving an illusion of a cooling breeze. They were not really necessary at this season but were indispensable in the summer months.

After the meal Andhra would have moved to the drawing room, but Ranjana forestalled her.

"I've arranged a small entertainment in the courtyard in honor of our first guests," he explained. "Bring wraps for the ladies, Imrat. It may be a little chilly sitting out there at this time."

Imrat soon returned with a couple of Kashmir shawls, and as she and Jenny draped them around their shoulders, Andhra said, "Do you remember how you used to entertain us in the old days, Jenny? You playing the piano, Father and I singing, and the dog howling in protest. What ages ago it seems."

Jenny nodded, her eyes moist, as Ranjana led the way to the courtyard, where four chairs were grouped at one end in front of a clear space on the marble floor.

As soon as they were seated, a troupe of musicians entered and took their places, seating themselves cross-legged on cushions piled at the back. Sitars, tablas, santoors, ghatoms, flutes and drums all began to tune up softly, and Andhra leaned back in pleasurable anticipation. How thoughtful of Ranjana to have arranged this surprise for them all.

But the music was only a preliminary. Suddenly there was a loud fanfare on the drums, and from behind a fretted sandalwood screen a dancer burst, bounding into the clearing in front of the musicians. She bowed to the prince and his guests with hands humbly folded before her face.

With a pang of annoyance Andhra saw that it was Rakhee. Why, with numerous others all eager for such engagements, had Ranjana chosen her?

The next moment she quelled her displeasure as being quite absurd. Rakhee was at the top of her profession, so naturally Ranjana had chosen the best for his guests, herself included.

Rakhee could certainly dance. Her sinewy body swayed and pulsated as though boneless. Arms and legs postured, bare feet thumped the floor, eyes flickered in a fantastic number of expressions within the painted framework of her long black lashes, while her girdled sari of blue and silver clung to her voluptuous figure in the most provocative way.

Andhra stole a glance at her husband. His interest was profound. At the moment he had eyes for no one else, and the way the pulse beat in his temples showed clearly the arousal of the hunter in him—the stirrings of primitive male instincts that could, unless gratified in some other way, lead to disaster.

Perturbed, her glance slid to the others to see if they, too, noticed.

Jenny was quite enthralled with this sensuous entertainment that never came her way up in British-dominated Darjeeling. She was utterly oblivious to the reactions of anyone else.

Robert Pearson was another matter. With a shock like a douche of cold water, she found his gaze concentrated on herself with the same earthy sentiments that Ranjana was displaying toward Rakhee.

Emotions were getting out of hand, she reflected as she hastily averted her glance. This primitive music and dancing, with roots going back through time, was too calculated to excite lusty young males. She must be firm and see to it that such entertainments did not occur too often. She would fight like a tigress to keep the exclusive love of her handsome prince.

CHAPTER THREE

Jenny had been at the palace for a full month, and tomorrow she was leaving to travel north to her own home in Darjeeling.

"You know I don't want to leave you, darling Andhra," she explained, "but Mark has been very patient and I don't feel I can neglect him any longer. I daresay his everyday needs like food and washing are taken care of, but husbands have other needs, don't they?"

"They certainly have. Wives, too." Andhra's thoughts leaped ahead with a surge of excitement to tonight. After this afternoon's ceremony in the temple and the public rejoicing later in the day, she would be free of restraint and could resume her normal life with Ranjana. With that as a bedrock, she would have no need to fear dancing girls or any other temptation cast her husband's way.

"Mark will be interested to know what progress has been made on the estate," Jenny went on. "Why don't we take a walk and I'll see firsthand how everything is going."

They were sitting at breakfast. Robert Pearson set down his coffee cup and glanced at her and Andhra.

"You're welcome. Come along with Ranjana and me. You'll be surprised at how much has already been accomplished."

He was staying in the palace until the bungalow that was being built for him on the plantation was ready. That would be quite soon now, small and simple as it was. Although she liked him, Andhra privately felt that it would be a good thing when he was no longer in such close proximity. It was clear to her that his feelings toward her were growing too ardent and, but for his typical English restraint, could become an embarrassment to them both. Ranjana, too, was becoming aware of it, and he occasionally resorted to untypical brusqueness in his dealings with the new manager.

But this was a festive day, and no jarring note marred it as yet. At the close of breakfast they all walked over the short bridge that connected the Summer Palace to the mainland and the estate.

The rolling hills about them made an exhilarating landscape. It would be quite beautiful when it was clothed with the attractive green of squat tea bushes, growing close together as in Darjeeling, with a few trees sprouting among them to give shade.

"The slopes aren't steep enough to require terracing, which will make the work of clearing, planting and, later, harvesting much easier," Robert explained.

A start had not yet been made on the lower ground nearest the palace. Here the huts and untidy plots of the coolies lay, the thatched shacks spilling naked children, chickens, pigs and goats. A few rice paddies showed intensely green between, interspersed with coconut and banana palms and small patches of spices, pineapples and coffee bushes.

"Eventually these will all have to go, and then, when tea completely takes over, the estate will really look good and be a flourishing concern," Ranjana explained for the benefit of Andhra and Jenny. "With around two thousand acres, it should yield a good profit besides giving regular work to a great many people. Tea plantations are very labor intensive, as with proper management the workers can be employed for most of the year on one job or another. And if other landowners are encouraged to set up in tea, south India, traditionally bordering on famine, could become much more prosperous."

His voice was confident, his expression full of fervor. He really cared about helping his people and his country, Andhra reflected with a glow of understanding. But did they appreciate it? They were ignorant, superstitious and tradition bound, with the flames of their resentment fanned by the seeds sown by Uncle Balbir. She very much doubted it.

The hostility was veiled as yet. None of these wretched people dared show anything but subservience to their prince. Pray heaven they would realize the benefits and ignore the sly insinuations of Nawab Balbir Mukti and accept these new conditions as time went by.

He would be coming this afternoon with his unattractive wife, Andhra remembered, pursing her lips. When she had questioned it with Ranjana, he had said, "Of course the family has been invited for the celebration of the birth of my son and heir. It would have caused unfavorable comment otherwise and an open breach between him and me. We can't aggravate an already delicate situation, my pearl."

They moved on through these small plots to higher ground. Here many coolies were at work, uprooting trees with the aid of working elephants, trained to obey and to cooperate. Other gangs cleared the debris to make way for the primitive wooden plows, pulled by oxen and steered by drivers walking behind, bellowing instructions.

When they came to a small, fenced patch already green with squat young tea bushes, Andhra stared in surprise. "Surely they haven't grown to this stage so soon?" she asked, turning to Robert.

He smiled. "I cheated a little by bringing some young bushes from the best of the bushes up north. They'll initiate the workers into their management and get us going. Tea bushes need a lot of care, you know. If left to their own devices they'd grow to a height of twenty-five feet and put all their energy into flowering. We can't let that happen, so we plant them very close together, as you see, and repeatedly prune them to induce luxuriant leaf growth."

Jenny nodded. "I do know a little about tea growing, living where I do. That only the delicate young shoots are picked, for instance, to keep the mellow flavor."

"That's right. These will take about two years before they are ready for plucking, and those growing from seed a little longer. We have some coming on in this patch, you see."

Andhra glanced at the tiny saplings. "You've certainly lost no time. Is that your bungalow? What a nice little home."

In the shade of a clump of coconut palms, with thatched roof, open veranda and several airy rooms, it was cool and inviting. Bamboo chairs, a charpoy bed and other simple furniture was being carried in and set on the coir-matting floor, while to the rear a well was being sunk.

"You can move in tomorrow and keep an eye on these young plants," Ranjana said, not troubling to hide his satisfaction.

Would he feel lonely after a month in the busy palace, Andhra wondered. Why had he never married some nice English girl up in Darjeeling and settled down there among his own kind? He was handsome and eligible enough, surely.

She broke off the train of thought, conscious that she should not be wondering about his private life at all. Ranjana was right. It was better that he move out of their family orbit immediately, before things got out of hand.

They climbed higher, through more ground being cleared, and finally came to the huts being built for the workers. There was row upon row of them—tiny, thatched, two-room dwellings for families, longer units of six single rooms for unattached males.

A gang of men was busy on these, thatching the roofs with great palm leaves tied neatly down with rope made from coir. These huts cost little to make—no more than fifty rupees each, Ranjana had declared, with all the raw materials free to hand and labor costs dirt cheap.

Shukur Thayar, the deposed manager, was in charge of this building work, at a fair wage. His status was nevertheless greatly reduced and his former ability to cream off some of the estate revenue into his own pocket curtailed, so his reaction was predictably sour. He would make mischief if and when he could, Andhra felt.

On every hand they seemed to have potential enemies. It was not an auspicious beginning, but they must simply make the best of it, and today of all days discordant thoughts must be thrust to the background. Today was a day of rejoicing.

Shukur Thayar answered the prince's greeting without enthusiasm.

"This afternoon is a holiday for all the hands," Ranjana informed him. "This evening there will be entertainment in the courtyard for all who care to come, and food and drink in plenty."

Shukur's thanks were somewhat surly. He never would forgive Ranjana for taking over here, installing a new manager, turning the estate into a tea plantation and forcing him to live in one of those coolie huts after the luxury of the palace.

After lunch Andhra dressed in a plain dark sari, veiled her head and face and set off for the temple in the little village of Nanassar on the edge of the estate. She rode in an enclosed rickshaw accompanied only by Mumtaz and baby Sanjay, the cause of all the ceremony. Jenny followed in another rickshaw, in charge of the clothes into which Andhra would change after the cleansing ritual.

The small village temple was a world apart from the sprawling stone edifices with their magnificent gopurams that dotted the countryside of south India. Built of wood and stucco, it was garishly painted, with garlands of marigolds and jasmine festooning its flanking images, and a strong perfume of burning oils and incense scenting the air.

Andhra set the temple bell jangling. Then, kicking off her shoes, she passed inside to the inner sanctuary, the shrine of Shiva and Parvati. Here the priest waited, chanting his ritual prayers, and here she kneeled, hands folded before her face, to be sprinkled with sacred flower petals and sweet-smelling powder. Rising, she walked to the back of the temple and down a flight of steps into the small sacred pool, where she immersed herself entirely in the cool water.

Mumtaz helped her out and hurried her into a small robing room, where Andhra's change of clothes had been deposited. Here the ayah pulled off the clinging wet sari and dressed her mistress in the sumptuous outfit waiting for her, afterward brushing out her gleaming black hair and braiding it into a shining crown. This she decked with fragrant jasmine flowers and completed the alluring effect with a wreath of marigolds and jasmine around Andhra's slender neck.

Now, in her flowing purple sari and gold sandals, Andhra looked every inch a princess. As she passed through, the priest pressed the red mark of distinction onto the golden skin of her brow, adding the last touch of elegance.

And there, seated in a howdah beneath a golden, fringed umbrella, waited Ranjana, in his superb ceremonial attire.

The elephant that bore him was equally magnificent, decked out in gorgeous trappings, his mahout or trainer sitting proudly on the great beast's neck beneath the flower-decked howdah.

The elephant kneeled at command. Andhra was helped up to sit behind her husband, while Mumtaz joined Jenny in her rickshaw and jealously took the *chota sahib* into her own arms, where he belonged.

Then, accompanied by musicians, with Ranjana's relatives and friends bringing up the rear on elephants or in rickshaws, the procession wended its slow way first around the village, where the inhabitants crowded to stare and cheer, and then through the estate, to give the prince's people a chance to see their new princeling, who would one day rule over them.

There was plenty of cheering and calls of *"namaste"* with hands raised before dark Tamil faces in the gesture of salutation. Andhra accepted it with a serene smile as befitted her rank, while privately speculating whether it was not more in anticipation of the feasting and entertainment to come rather than any real enthusiasm for this stranger from the north, Prince Ranjana, and his family, who neither knew nor respected the easygoing traditional ways of the south.

Riding high on the elephant in the pleasant warmth of the late-afternoon winter sun, they wended their way along the dusty track, fringed by trees freshened by the late monsoon into sporadic growth. Tall, gray-trunked eucalyptus towered over the strange casuarinas, aerial-rooted banyans and graceful fan palms, until the plots of the estate people took over with their more domestic crops of coffee, pineapples, bananas and the small, sweet oranges of the south.

At last the bridge was reached that separated the island and the Summer Palace from the sprawling estate. Andhra, a little tired now, was glad to dismount, knowing that the most exacting part of this day was over.

But there could be no relaxing yet. She and Jenny, with Mumtaz and the baby, must now leave the men to their separate feast and take their place in the women's quarters of the palace, to lounge on cushions and divans with Uncle Balbir's fat wife, Madhumita, and other distant female relations or friends attending the ceremony. Here they were served great bowls of rice and curry on squat tables, eaten as a matter of course with the fingers, which Andhra, grown used to Western ways, now hated as much as Jenny did. When she and Ranjana were alone, she would sweep away all these ancient customs, she had decided. They would eat together in their small, newly furnished dining room and afterward retire to the drawing room to spend their leisure as they pleased. No doubt the servants would disapprove and whisper about this unorthodox behavior, but they would not dare to show their feelings too openly.

But for the moment she must make stilted conversation with these alien beings and allow little Sanjay to be passed from one to another, to be patted and cooed over and declared a fine baby.

At last it was over. The company had stuffed themselves with rich sweets dripping with honey and nuts and drunk cup after cup of thick sweet coffee, washed their hands in the finger bowls and were ready to join the men in the courtyard for the entertainment.

A dais had been erected at one end of the spacious court-yard, banked with flowers and potted plants. In front of it rich Oriental rugs were laid down, dotted with cushions. Andhra, Ranjana, Jenny, Uncle Balbir and the rest of the family took their places in the front row, sitting cross-legged as a matter of course, while the other guests seated themselves behind. Then as many of the estate workers as could crowd into the remaining space pushed and thrust their way in to fill up the rear and watch a performance by the Kathakali dancers, a traditional entertainment of south India that was greatly relished by the masses.

Privately Andhra thought little of it. The elaborate dresses of the all-male cast were a little too lurid for her taste, while the fantastic face makeup she found almost frightening.

With the musicians adding suitable side effects and giving them their cues, the small cast began their miming. The theme was the eventual triumph of good over evil, the good leaving no doubt of their identity with their vivid green faces, while the temptress and the villains were of darker shades.

The play ended to loud applause and stamping of bare feet

by the estate workers, after which came a succession of dances by various artists. Jenny and Andhra enjoyed these very much until the last one, when Andhra was annoyed to see Rakhee bound onto the stage to round off the performance with her celebrated solo.

She was in her most seductive mood, posturing and leaping in fantastic poses and making great play with her mobile face and eyes directly in front of Ranjana. Andhra, seated next to him, could sense his rising tide of passion and could cheerfully have watched some accident befall the dancer so that she would be forced to retire.

Casting an appraising glance at Balbir, Andhra saw that he was aware of Rakhee's interest and sat glowering at her and Ranjana alike. The incident was certain to wipe out any good-will engendered by the celebration meal and fan the flame of Balbir's jealousy, for not only had this upstart nephew inherited what he felt should be his, but he had now stolen the interest of his favorite dancing girl.

It was a great relief when the entertainment finished, to the thunder of drums, and Rakhee retired.

Now was the time for the prince and his guests to leave the courtyard to the coolies and their families. Here the remains of the feast enjoyed earlier by the dignitaries would be brought, and for once the workers could eat their fill of the goodies.

Andhra touched her husband's hand briefly as they rose, to bring his attention back to her. He clasped it firmly, and his eyes lost their sultry gleam and became warm and intimate for her alone. With a throb of joy she thought of tonight, when Rakhee would have to be content with Balbir's attentions, while she would at last have her incomparable prince, after all these months of enforced abstinence.

But first custom decreed that the men get together again to drink coffee and talk, while the women went to their quarters to do the same or retire for the night, as they pleased.

Madhumita, tired by the long day, fortunately decided to retire. The rest of the women followed suit, and Andhra and Jenny were glad to seek their respective rooms also after the excitement of the day.

Andhra dismissed the ayah to go and watch over Sanjay in

the small night nursery he now occupied. She locked the outer door with a sigh of relief and cast off her sumptuous sari and flashing jewels, then took a refreshing bath in the stand-up bathtub, ladling over herself the warm water Mumtaz had brought up.

Greatly refreshed, she freely used the scented oil perfumed with flowers to make her body beautiful for Ranjana, then slipped on a diaphanous night robe.

His bedroom was next door. She took care that the connecting door was unlocked, then climbed into the great canopied bed. Intricately carved and painted, it had stood in the palace for decades, but Andhra had installed a British-style feather bed to make a soft nest. On this she settled herself, leaving the mosquito net folded neatly on the top frame until Ranjana's arrival.

The evening was warm enough as yet to dispense with any cover. Relaxed and drowsy from her bath, she lay quiet, wishing that she could hear his quick movements next door, see his longed-for figure standing beside her. But he must first do his duty and wait until the male guests retired.

He was a long time. She could imagine his impatience as etiquette demanded that he make polite conversation with his guests to the sound of monotonous Indian background music and tell them of his plans for the estate. In spite of her longing, Andhra's eyelids drooped, and soon her gentle, regular breathing showed that she slept.

Was it a dream, the hands that moved seductively over the diaphanous gown, touching every inch of her and bringing a gasp of desire. No dream, for when her eyes fluttered open, it was to encounter the lithe naked form of her darling Ranjana bending over her.

"Beloved," he murmured hoarsely, "it seems a lifetime since I came to you thus and we were as one being. Now all the frustration is behind us."

With a lightninglike, almost-savage movement, he tore off the flimsy wrap and flung it to the floor, gazing down with quickened breath at her golden-skinned beautiful form lying invitingly beneath him.

"As slim and as perfect as before Sanjay's birth," he murmured, his gaze lingering on the pink tips of her full breasts, the delicate curve of her hips, the secret places that only he knew. "My beloved, my pearl of great price, it is as though we were coming together for the first time. Do you remember the caves of Elephanta Island?"

"As though I could ever forget!"

Her hand grasped his, drawing him to her. With one lithe movement he was beside her, the mosquito net was drawn behind him, and the intimate enclosure became again the temple of divine eroticism that Shiva himself would have looked upon with indulgent approval.

dishes, but Jenny preferred the British food she and Mark ate in Darjeeling and merely picked at the many little pots on her tray. Andhra felt glad that she had instructed the cook to prepare a packed basket of chicken, rolls and fruit for her sister to take on her journey north.

Jenny would be greatly missed, but Andhra would be glad to see the back of Uncle Balbir and his family, as well as the rest of the guests. They were all leaving today, and she could look forward to a normal routine, with Ranjana and Sanjay the center of her world.

But they had scarcely finished the meal than there came an interruption. Shukur Thayar, the deposed manager of the estate, was shown in. He was in a great state of excitement.

"Much trouble, Your Highness," he exclaimed after a perfunctory greeting of *"namaste."* "There is a man-eating tiger in the neighborhood. He must have had his lair in the wild edge of the estate bordering the hill jungle, and was disturbed by the plowing up of the land to make way for this ill-starred tea plantation. We have destroyed his natural food supply and his lair, so now he will destroy us!"

Ranjana sprang to his feet. "What has happened? Explain yourself quickly."

"This morning a child was pounced on and killed when he went to the river for water. His mother heard a scream, but when she rushed down, she found only the water pot and a trail of disturbed undergrowth where the beast had dragged the boy off. When others went to investigate, there in the soft mud by the river were the huge marks of a tiger."

"That is bad. We must organize a hunt. Once he has tasted human blood he'll be back," Ranjana said, frowning.

"That is so, Highness. There have also been several cattle killed lately. We did not know the cause until now. He is cunning and vicious, this tiger."

A strange excitement had come over Uncle Balbir at these tidings of woe. Andhra intercepted a glance between him and his son Satish that seemed pregnant with hidden meaning. He now lifted his hand in a gesture of command.

"There is no time to be lost. We must act immediately if further lives or cattle are not to be sacrificed. I have had more

CHAPTER FOUR

The world was a beautiful place, Andhra reflected with a sigh of pure happiness as she stretched her golden, naked body like a sleek kitten and slid from the bed. In the bathroom next door she could hear the sounds of Ranjana taking his morning ablutions. She would have unconcernedly joined him but for the fact that the singsong voice of Jaykar, his manservant, proved that he was not alone. She could hear the sound of water as Jaykar ladled it over his master's head with the small dipper that was part of every Indian bathroom. Now he would be standing with the open bath towel, waiting to slip it around the sinewy form of the young prince and towel him dry. Absurdly, she felt almost jealous of the middle-aged Tamil who seemed to have become devotedly attached to his master. Almost as devoted as Mumtaz was to her. With a rueful smile Andhra acknowledged that they were the only two in thi lovely, rambling dwelling whom she felt she could really trus

Now Jaykar was assisting his master to dress, and soon ther was silence, Andhra's cue to go in for her own quick dip.

The warm water cans were empty. Mumtaz would ha commanded more to be brought had she been here, but Ar hra had expressly bidden her to devote most of her time little Sanjay. It was no hardship to splash herself with c water, which was never quite cold here and brought a c cious sense of exhilaration to her golden body.

Presently, dressed, she went down to breakfast, taken n the dining room with Ranjana but with their guests in or the older rooms today. It was a typical Indian meal, consi of rice, hot Madras curry, yogurt and an assortment of s sauces, served to each guest on a large round tray with p chapatties to mop up the mush. Andhra was quite used to experience than you in the matter of arranging tiger shoots, Ranjana. I shall postpone my departure for a few days and send for Prem, my trusted *shikari*. He is an expert at hunting and a deadly shot."

Andhra bit her lip. So she must endure his company and that of his family for a while longer. But of course so menacing an animal must be tracked down and killed.

"I'll give orders for a *macham* to be built at once," Ranjana said, looking toward Robert Pearson, who was breakfasting with them, not yet having moved into his new bungalow. "It is the surest way of killing a man-eater."

A *macham* was a tall shooting platform, built at the scene of the tiger's last kill and hidden as much as possible with creepers and greenery, Andhra reflected. Bait in the form of a living animal was usually tethered nearby, and the marksmen waited patiently in the *macham* until the quarry showed up, sometimes all night. It was a rather tame way of bagging a kill, so it was seldom resorted to in the way of sport but frequently done in a desperate situation like this.

Uncle Balbir clicked his tongue impatiently. "*Machams* may be all right for timid white sahibs, nephew, but not for such as you and I. We shall hunt and kill the beast in the time-honored princely fashion, on elephant back, with experienced *shikaris* surrounding us. That way offers good sport and keeps up our prestige in the eyes of the people. Are you a coward to talk of *machams?*"

Ranjana's eyes flashed fire. Clearly his uncle had taken advantage of his age and relationship. "No man casts doubts on my courage! So be it, if that is the way you want it. We shall stalk and hunt with elephants!" he said curtly. "You and Shukur organize things between you, since he is more used to these things." He had turned to Robert Pearson.

Shukur Thayar oozed importance. It was a long time since he had been credited with authority. "The elephant stable is somewhat depleted, Highness, but a few can be mustered with outside help," he declared. "Leave everything to me."

"You may organize the elephants, beaters and *shikaris*, but I shall take charge of the actual hunt," Uncle Balbir declared. "We shall set forth an hour before dawn tomorrow morning, in the hope of catching the tiger coming down to the river to drink. Since your elephants are in short supply, my *shikari* shall bring his own, and his mahout to load his gun. Prem will not fail you."

Robert Pearson and Shukur Thayar set off to get the hunt organized, while Uncle Balbir dispatched his son Satish to their own palace down in Cochpur, to bring back the promised help. His wife, Madhumita, plump and sluggish through overindulgence in sticky sweetmeats of nuts and honey, went off to the *zenara* or women's quarter of the palace, her ayah trailing after her, neither of them too pleased by this enforced delay here.

Andhra, as slim and vital as they were fat and slow, was in no mood to dance attendance on them and miss all the excitement. She grasped her husband's arm as he was about to stalk off to see for himself that everything was being organized to the best advantage.

"I want to go with you tomorrow morning. I've never yet been on a tiger hunt. Do say I might sit in your howdah. I'm used to guns and can load for you, or even shoot myself if necessary."

He looked doubtful. Before he could answer, Uncle Balbir broke in harshly. "It is not the custom for women to hunt. They could be a hindrance and a danger to themselves and the party."

Andhra's nostrils flared. "Nonsense! I can shoot as well as most men, and have as much nerve, too. Among the British Raj in the north, it is quite commonplace for the ladies to accompany a shoot. So the sooner I set the custom down here the better. I don't intend to live in purdah, whatever the other women do."

Balbir muttered something contemptuously under his breath, but Ranjana had eyes for none save his wife. How captivatingly beautiful she was since the birth of their child— like an exotic flower opened in full bloom to the warmth of the sun.

"How can I deny you anything after last night, my pearl of great price. Come with me if you wish," he murmured fondly.

Balbir walked off in frustrated ill temper. What a blessing it would be when he had taken himself home and they were left in exquisite privacy, they each reflected.

She saw little more of Ranjana that day. He was out on the far boundary of the estate, inspecting the region where the tiger lurked, helping in the arrangements for the forthcoming shoot, urging the estate workers to stay within their homes from dusk onward and to safeguard their livestock. They needed little urging. Past experience had taught them the grim reality of a man-eater at large, and none would breathe freely until the menace was exterminated.

They did all meet at dinner, but with Balbir and his family still present, there was an irksome constraint. Satish had returned with Prem, his father's head *shikari,* a splendid specimen of an elephant, and the mahout. They were all housed in the elephant stables and living quarters, along with the palace elephants that were being prepared for the shoot.

Andhra, in consideration of the very early start, retired immediately after dinner. Mumtaz had laid out her riding habit and boots and a tray of light refreshments, but Andhra was too keyed up to eat when she rose by lamplight the next morning and pulled on her clothes. Taking only a drink, she joined Ranjana and Robert Pearson, the latter carrying several guns.

It was cool outside, with a faint mist rising from the lake. This would disperse at sunup and the heat gradually take over, as it did without fail during this dry season of the year.

They swiftly crossed the bridge to the sprawling estate and walked silently past the sleeping families in their two-room thatched huts, up the slope that would soon be clothed in squat green tea bushes, to the wild land that bordered the jungle. Once choked with undergrowth and various trees all battling for light and air, it was now churned up and being made ready for cultivation, except for a narrow strip adjoining the river, which divided the estate from the jungle.

Here the tiger had made his kill, and here were waiting a number of elephants at strategic points, with *shikaris* concealed in the undergrowth, their guns at the ready.

Uncle Balbir and his son Satish occupied a howdah on one elephant. Andhra and Ranjana mounted another, while Robert Pearson joined Shukur Thayar on his great beast close by.

"We shall not use the beaters yet. Hopefully the tiger will come down to the river to drink and seek the same easy kill as he had yesterday morning when he pounced on the child," Balbir said. "If he takes the bait, we'll all aim for him at once, and surely one of our shots will finish him."

The bait was a young bullock tethered at the edge of the river, unconcernedly cropping the vegetation. At strategic points, concealed as much as possible by the lush river growth yet within sight and shot of the bait, the elephants took up their stand.

From the deep silence of night, the jungle on the far side of the river slowly began to stir into life. High above, gray succeeding black heralded the dawn. The harsh cry of a peacock answered by the more cheerful call of a jungle fowl rang out through the chill of early morning, warning them to be on guard. This was the most likely time to catch their quarry, though all knew that a tiger was an unpredictable creature, hunting by day or night as the mood took him.

Time passed. Both humans and elephants grew tired of standing motionless, but they persisted until the sun shone brassily from the sky and the whole jungle rang with the calls of monkeys frolicking in the treetops, parakeets flashing gaudily among the creepers and vines, smaller animals going about their business in the dank, dim recesses enclosed by the crowded vegetation across the river.

Mosquitoes and other insects buzzed around, biting mercilessly. Andhra was very glad she had plastered her face with a concoction guaranteed to repel these unwelcome advances, made by Mumtaz from wild plants. It certainly worked in her case.

"The tiger isn't going to show up this morning," Ranjana said at last. "Not unless we hunt him out. I'm sorry you've been disappointed, my love, but I half expected as much."

Balbir realized the same thing. He plodded over on his elephant, his blotched, bitten face looking quite sour. "We'll send out the *shikaris* to track him down. Then the beaters can force him this way," he declared.

The *shikaris* set off, as silent and watchful as panthers, followed by the small party on elephants. The beaters brought up the rear, all moving with the utmost care.

Balbir's head man did eventually find the tiger's pug marks in soft ground, but the efforts of the beaters failed to force the quarry into the open. At last, frustrated, hungry and angry with his uncle, Ranjana called a halt.

"Enough of this showmanship! We are not hunting reserved tiger for sport but a cunning and deadly man-eater," he said angrily. "All this display only serves to put him on guard. Now I shall do it my own way, but for today we must call a halt. The beast will not show up now."

Balbir brushed aside Ranjana's assertion that he could handle the situation without his help. "I shall remain with you until the killer is brought down," he insisted. "But we shall try your way, with *machams*. We shall build two—one on either side of the bait. Satish and I shall man one, you and Pearson the other. That way we'll be less detectable than on elephant back with a crowd about us."

"Precisely what I suggested at first!" Ranjana declared in disgust as they walked back to the palace.

Andhra was silent, deep in thought. Why was Balbir so determined to stay? She had no illusions that it was from the goodness of his heart that he wanted to help rid them of the menace, so he must have some ulterior motive.

Conjecture as to what this could be filled her with deep unease. She would have preferred to mention it to her husband, but they had no chance before dinner. Afterward they were both tired and fell asleep in each other's arms as soon as their love had been satisfied.

The following morning it became clear how right Ranjana had been in his estimation of the tiger's cunning, for on rising, the news was brought that another victim had been seized. A young man had gone down to the river to water his buffaloes at a deep pool and been pounced on and dragged off by the brute. The trail of blood had been clearly visible when members of his family had gone to investigate his absence.

Ranjana gave orders for two *machams* to be built, one on each side of the spot where the man-eater had struck last. Fortunately a couple of wild mango trees grew about fifty yards apart, which would save a lot of work. In these two rough platforms were constructed and furnished with blankets in case an all-night vigil was necessary.

As there was a possibility of catching the beast at sundown if he came to the river to drink at the water hole, they decided to have an early dinner, then go to the river immediately afterward.

Andhra, still hoping to see her first tiger at close quarters, donned her safari suit and set off with them, in spite of Uncle Balbir's objections. He insisted on taking Prem, his *shikari,* along, and also his mahout to keep watch down below and give them the signal should the quarry show up.

With Ranjana's help, Andhra climbed nimbly up to the *macham,* and settled herself on a rug, her back against the trunk of the tree. Ranjana and Robert Pearson squatted in front of her on the sturdy bamboo platform. They must keep on the alert, however long the vigil should last. A young buffalo had been tethered to act as bait on their side of the river.

It was a likely spot to catch a tiger coming down to drink, Ranjana explained in a low tone. The mango tree branches overhung the deep, rocky pool, and in the soft ground adjoining, a track of pug marks was clearly visible. Most of the leaves around the platform had been stripped away to give the watchers a clearer view, and at a height of fifteen feet, Andhra felt quite safe.

It was now dusk, and the jungle across the river was beginning to stir into evening activity.

"The tiger won't be so easy to spot if he comes after dark," Andhra whispered. "At least not until he's right beneath us."

"Don't worry," Robert murmured. "There's a full moon tonight. It will be almost as bright as daylight."

In their close proximity his hand brushed hers, either intentionally or by accident. Andhra suspected the former. There was no doubt in her mind that he was deeply in love with her. It came over in off-guard glances, the odd word, the small attentions, such as bringing her flowers, that he paid her. Fortunately Ranjana noticed nothing, though she had a nagging suspicion that the servants, with their usual sixth sense, were not so trustingly blind.

Nothing could ever come of it, of course. Her love for her husband was too great ever to be challenged, but Andhra wished she could find some way of warning Robert off without hurting his feelings, for his own sake. She liked him too much to see him hurt.

She glanced at the second *macham*, a little way along the river, in which Balbir and Satish were sitting. Did they notice, with their lynx eyes? If so, they would try to make mischief out of it sooner or later. Once again she wished they were gone from the palace.

By eight o'clock it would have been pitch dark but for the moon that was now rising, a shining orb over the jungle. As their hope of the tiger showing up at dusk had not material-ized, they must now settle down to wait with all the patience they could muster. At the moment it was still comfortably warm, but as the night advanced they would have need of their blankets against the creeping cold, they were all well aware. Andhra recalled the tales she had heard of several weary nights spent in vigil before a man-eater was finally caught, and fervently hoped that this would not happen on this occasion.

In spite of her keyed-up state, she actually fell into a doze, knowing that two alert men were on guard. It must have lasted a long time, for when some sixth sense roused her, the radiant moon had set and the dawn was breaking with a cold, gray light.

An electric tenseness in the attitude of the two men told her that they had heard something. They sat like temple images, every sense keyed to its highest pitch.

Straining her ears, she heard it, too—a grunting, coughing sound—and knew that their quarry was about to show up. It came from the jungle in a spot just across the river from where the tiger had snatched his last victim.

Then there came the softly muffled yet heavy tread of a large body in the fallen bamboo leaves of the jungle, followed by a thud as a great tawny creature leaped across the narrow, rocky bed of the river adjoining the pool and landed on the ground just beside the terrified buffalo, midway between the two *machams*.

The buffalo let out a bellow of fear, that could not fail to arouse Balbir and Satish even had they been dozing. With their guns trained on the tiger from one side and Ranjana and Robert shooting from opposite angles, the tiger was surely doomed.

Ranjana, without making the slightest sound to give away his presence and send the quarry bounding back into the jungle, was bending forward and downward as far as he could without falling from his perch, the muzzle of his gun pointing at the tawny beast as it leaped on the buffalo to bring it to its knees. Just as the gleaming fangs buried themselves in the victim's neck, Ranjana prepared to pull the trigger and make a killing shot into the savage head.

Then two things happened simultaneously. From a concealing thorn bush below Balbir's *macham* the figure of Prem, his *shikari,* thrust itself forward, gun raised. At the same moment Robert, huddled close beside Ranjana, also leaned forward to fire his own gun, knowing that the prince's shot might only wound the writhing, snarling target locked in combat with the buffalo.

Andhra's hand flew to her mouth. A startled gasp escaped her as her glance fell on the unexpected sight of Prem, his gun pointing not at the man-eater but directly at her husband.

Neither Robert nor Ranjana had eyes for anything save their target, and Andhra's alarm was too late to warn them, for even as they fired together at the tiger, Prem's gun spat out in their direction.

Two further shots followed from Balbir and Satish, masking the cry of pain wrung from Robert Pearson. All eyes being on the tiger now writhing in its death throes, only Andhra noticed Robert's contorted face and saw him clutch at his left leg.

"You're wounded!" she said in concern, and then in mounting anger. "It was the *shikari!* I distinctly saw him pointing his gun up here."

Robert laughed shakily. "Why should he do that? You must have been mistaken. No doubt the bullet was meant for the tiger, but in the excitement of the moment it missed its mark and flew over here."

"An experienced *shikari* shouldn't make such a glaring mistake as that, but we'll leave that for the moment. Our first task is to get you down and home to medical attention," she declared.

Ranjana now became aware of this unexpected development. "How, by all the gods, did *you* manage to get hurt?" he asked in astonishment.

"It was Prem! I realize it all now," Andhra said. "*You* were the intended target, but Robert leaned in front of you at the crucial moment, to get better aim at the tiger. The bullet got him instead of you."

Blood now began to seep through the khaki drill of Robert's trousers. Sweat broke out on his brow, and pallor showed beneath his tan.

"We need help! Come over here," Ranjana roared.

Balbir and Satish scrambled down and, together with Prem, ran over.

"What kind of *shikari* do you employ that he shoots my manager through the leg?" Ranjana asked angrily. "We were nowhere near the tiger."

Prem loudly began to voice his sorrow and his innocence of evil intent. "It was the huge size of the beast," he declared. "Never have I seen such a one. The excitement made my hand shake and my aim false."

"That's not the only false thing," Andhra said in disgust.

Between them they lowered Robert to the ground, made a rough litter from bamboo poles lashed with vines and carried the wounded man back to the palace. A servant was dispatched for the estate doctor, who lived in the adjoining village. He was not highly qualified but possessed an inborn skill. He soon extracted the bullet and made the victim comfortable.

"The tiger is dead, and for that I'm glad, Nephew," Balbir declared. "Yet I leave you in sorrow and contrition, because my *shikari* has accidentally deprived you of the services of your new manager."

Lying hypocrite, Andhra reflected, her eyes flashing fire. She felt quite certain that he had planned it all and had instructed Prem to fire at Ranjana. He had meant the prince to be killed so that he might stake a claim to the Summer Palace. He must be seething inwardly that the plan had misfired and only the new manager been put out of action for a time. Yet even that was to his advantage, for now Shukur Thayar would have to take over again, another crook as deep and devious as Balbir himself. No doubt he would keep Balbir informed of all that went on in the palace after he had left and stir up trouble if he could.

Across the room her glance, full of indignant hatred, met that of Balbir, turned in her direction. It was equally hostile, a cold, calculating hostility that confirmed what an implacable enemy he was. His resentment of Ranjana and herself was too deep ever to die. He would scheme and plot against them as long as he lived for the unforgivable crime of taking the Summer Palace from under his very nose.

From now on it was strong-arm tactics with no holds barred.

CHAPTER FIVE

How feverish Robert Pearson looked when Andhra went into his room the following day carrying a glass of fresh pineapple juice and a vase of marigolds and jasmine freshly picked from the garden. Two spots of color burned in his tanned face, and his eyes glittered too brightly.

Was the local Tamil doctor any good for anything more serious than everyday complaints, she wondered fleetingly. He had probably received no scientific training but picked up all he knew from fakirs and folklore.

The sick man raised a smile at her approach. "Ah, the ministering angel," he said. "You're a sight to gladden the heart of any invalid, but I hate to put you to all this trouble. It seems wrong for a princess to be waiting on the plantation manager."

She smiled in return. "Between the two of us, I don't feel like a princess in spite of this great palace. I guess I lived too long as an army officer's daughter, in much humbler circumstances. I find being surrounded by so many servants somewhat irksome. I also fear they find me most unconventional and strongly disapprove of my Western outlook and emancipated ways."

"They'll almost certainly disapprove of your waiting on me," he said ruefully.

"Let them. Left entirely to their ministrations, you'd probably get short shrift. They're unctuous enough in dealing with us, but none of them willingly performs any but his own specified tasks. And apart from Mumtaz and Ranjana's valet, Jaykar, I don't believe we can really trust one of them. There's been too much insidious poison doled out against us by Uncle Balbir."

Robert nodded. "He's certainly a thorn in your flesh, and hand and glove with Shukur Thayar. The latter, of course, will

be reveling in my absence from authority and fervently wishing it could be permanent so that he could take over again on
the estate. Now if he'd been wielding the gun that caused it, I'd
have been inclined to think he did it on purpose."

Andhra's expression hardened. "Don't you see—that bullet
was meant for Ranjana. It was fired by the *shikari,* under
Balbir's instructions. He swears it was an accident and that he
was aiming for the tiger when a parrot flew in front of him,
distorting his aim. Both he and Balbir know very well that
nothing can be proved against him, but Ranjana and I are
certain that's the way it was. You see now how very thankful I
am that you were so close to Ranjana on the *macham* and just
happened to lean in front of him at the crucial moment. It's
certain that you saved him from injury and probably from
death. At the same time, I'm dreadfully sorry that you've had
to bear the brunt of what was meant for him. That's why I feel
bound to do all I can to show my gratitude."

He touched her slender, golden fingers consolingly. "It was
pure chance, but even had I known the consequences, I should
still have tried to protect Ranjana for your sake, my dear. I
know how much he means to you."

This was dangerous talk. He should not use endearments or
touch her hand so affectionately, even when they were alone,
she reflected uneasily. The servants were so unobtrusive. They
came and went like silent ghosts, so that they were almost part
of the furniture, and one was scarcely aware of them. And
having few interests in life, every little incident of palace life
was seized and gossiped about, usually with exaggeration,
which, in a situation like this, could lead to trouble. Ranjana
was the most loving of husbands, but perhaps because of it was
jealously possessive of her and would be quick to resent any
other man's desire of her, however well guarded.

Glancing up from her reflections, she was dismayed to see
that Shukur Thayar had silently entered and was regarding
them with an enigmatic, expressionless countenance. She hastily withdrew her hand from Robert's and strove to suppress the
flush mounting in her cheeks, more of anger against the deposed manager than guilt.

"It is customary in the Western world for a servant to knock before entering a private room," she said cuttingly. "How long will it take for you all to understand that?"

"A thousand pardons, Princess, but this is the East, not the West. What does it matter what a servant sees, if there is nothing to hide?"

His insolence fanned her vexation. With difficulty she checked her recriminations. Harping on it would only blow the incident out of proportion and incite him to make the most of it when he passed on the juicy tidbit to his cronies.

"What precisely do you want?" she demanded.

"I came to ask for the keys of the stores from Pearson sahib," he said smoothly, "so that I may carry on in his absence."

"Then I'll leave you to discuss work matters with him, but don't stay more than five minutes. He's ill and feverish following the removal of the bullet from his thigh and needs plenty of rest."

Without a further glance at Robert, she left the room, to encounter Ranjana as she was closing the door.

He stopped short in surprise. "I was about to see for myself how Robert is this morning, but I see you have beaten me to it. No doubt your motive was of the highest, my love, but think what the servants might make of it in this convention-bound atmosphere," he said. "Scandalous gossip would circle the palace like a forest fire if you were seen entering the estate manager's bedroom alone. Like Caesar's wife, you must be above suspicion at all times."

Coming from him, this was hard to take. He was right, of course, but that did not make things easier. After her English upbringing and the stark realities of the mutiny that she had lived through, it was irksome in the extreme to live in the narrow confines of a luxurious goldfish bowl.

"I'm afraid I've already put my foot in it as far as Shukur Thayar is concerned," she said tersely. "He's in there with Robert now. It's too much to take when one can't minister to a sick friend without exciting unfavorable gossip, especially as he's probably just saved your life."

"True, and I'm greatly indebted to him. Nevertheless, it will be easier for us all when he is no longer living with us in the palace itself. We'll hope he can be moved to his new house very soon, with a servant to care for his needs. How did you find him this morning?"

"With a high fever. I'm wondering if that Tamil doctor is competent enough for a serious case."

"Oh, they're usually surprisingly skilled. They use a lot of herbal and natural remedies and seem to know by instinct what to do. I don't think you need worry about the outcome in Robert's case."

"That's a mercy. Then I'll go up and see little Sanjay. I seem to have been neglecting him lately."

During the next few days the fever did subside, and against Andhra's judgment, Robert was installed in his new home on the estate, with his own bearer, a Tamil boy, to look after him. Privately she doubted whether the sick man would receive the full attention he needed, for the leg wound would confine him to bed for some time, leaving him fully dependent on this inexperienced youth. In spite of any eyebrows it might raise, Andhra resolved to keep an eye on him and his welfare, if only because of the indebtedness she felt toward him.

With Robert's enforced absence from the daily running of the estate, Ranjana was kept extra busy. Knowing Shukur Thayar to be easygoing, without scruples and quite ignorant of tea growing, Ranjana could not relax his supervision during this crucial stage in the young plants' development. He was determined that the project must succeed, if only to confound Uncle Balbir and all the other skeptics who prophesied failure simply because tea had never been grown before in this region.

"Since these hill slopes are similar to the hill country of Ceylon, where tea is grown successfully, it is logical to expect the same results here," Ranjana declared. "By all the gods, I mean to make it work, since coffee is too subject to the blight of *Hemileia vastatrix* to be depended upon on a large scale. Besides which, tea can be grown at a higher altitude than coffee and so will use our entire estate, giving employment to more coolies, which heaven knows they need."

Andhra heartily agreed. Plucking tea could be carried on almost all year around, each bush yielding a fresh crop of succulent young tips every seven to ten days. It was far more labor intensive than the sporadic work entailed in coffee growing.

Yet the estate coolies did not seem to appreciate this. They were suspicious, sullen and resentful of being turned out of their insanitary slum shacks and housed in the new long thatched huts, or attractive, two-room dwellings. Both Andhra and Ranjana were convinced that Shukur Thayar, egged on by Uncle Balbir, was slyly poisoning the atmosphere and bolstering their discontent with base innuendos against their new ruler and his grandiose plans.

Fortunately, in these early stages the young plants flourished. A brief, belated southwest monsoon made the best possible conditions in which to plant cuttings and seeds. The soil, deficient in zinc, was well sprayed with zinc sulphate, and every measure that Robert considered necessary was taken to ensure against failure.

Ranjana called on him frequently in his new bungalow to discuss progress and obtain guidance from the only tea expert on the estate.

"I'll be glad when he's out and about again," Ranjana confessed one morning when the brassy sun was already an enemy in the sky to be feared and shunned. "The hot season is upon us, and the young plants will need great care in watering to bring them healthily through it. Shukur Thayar toadies around when I'm in the vicinity and makes great play of being in charge and giving orders, but I'm sure he slacks off the moment my back is turned."

"Robert's wound seems to be taking an unusually long time to heal," Andhra said with a worried frown. "I never did think much of that Tamil doctor. He might have been better off in a Madras hospital."

Ranjana shrugged impatiently. The situation was clearly having an adverse effect on his usual equanimity. "He's on his feet at last, thank the gods, and hobbling around his bungalow on crutches. He's easily tired and can only keep going for short periods as yet, but I'm hopeful that he'll soon be able to get out and take charge again."

"I wonder if that bearer is looking after him properly," Andhra went on, all her maternal instincts coming to the fore.

"Why not? In any case, he's not your responsibility. I won't have you running after him and endangering your reputation, my love. Do remember how different the conventions are in southern India from your more liberal upbringing, and don't add to an already difficult situation."

Andhra seethed inwardly and had to bite her lower lip to keep back a scathing retort. Incredible though it appeared, a widening gulf seemed to have arisen between them on the subject of Robert. In the face of her indebtedness and gratitude to him for saving Ranjana from harm, it was difficult not to openly show it in any way possible.

As though fate was on her side, Ranjana felt bound by convention to pay a visit to Cochpur Palace that afternoon. It was the twenty-first birthday of Satish, Uncle Balbir's favorite son, and a day of feasting and rejoicing. The invitation had naturally included Andhra, but her disinclination to mix with them all again made her glad of an excuse.

"Little Sanjay was fretful for most of last night. I don't think the hot weather agrees with him," she explained. "As Mumtaz was kept awake, I promised her I would take care of the baby for two or three hours this afternoon while she slept, so I have a legitimate reason for staying at home. You can apologize for my absence."

He shrugged. "We have other servants."

"None I should care to leave in charge of Sanjay at his tender age."

So Ranjana set off alone on his splendid horse as soon as lunch was over, while Andhra settled the baby in his magnificent new carriage made of bamboo and lined with satin. It boasted a fringed canopy to keep off the sun and big spoked wheels to make movement easy. It had been specially made in Madras, and its like had never before been seen in these parts.

An outing in the fresh air, if it could be called fresh in this heat, might help the child to sleep better tonight, she decided.

It was then that the idea of going to see for herself how Robert was progressing entered her mind. She might as well walk toward his bungalow as any other way. True, the way was uphill, but the beaten earth track was firm enough to take wheeled vehicles easily and fringed by tall eucalyptus trees and casuarinas that cast a welcome shade for most of the way.

In her gauzy blue sari, its scarf thrown over her gleaming black hair for protection, she set out, quite ignoring the curious stares of the *dhobi wallah* setting off for the river, a pile of washing on his head.

How marvelous it felt to be entirely on her own, pushing her own pram, instead of relegating the task to Mumtaz with a bearer marching solemnly behind to uphold the dignity of the *chota sahib*.

The *bheesti*, shuffling around the environs of the palace, sprinkling water from his goatskin bag to lay the dust, moved deferentially from her way with a mumbled apology. He, too, stared curiously at the marvelous baby carriage and the amazing spectacle of the princess pushing it herself, without even an attendant ayah.

Smiling to herself, she crossed the bridge.

The dilapidated shacks with their small plots of land that had earlier covered the estate were now all swept away. Instead, immature tea plants sprouted close together, dotted here and there by palm trees that had been left standing to give some shade. Coolies worked in small groups with their primitive implements, keeping down the weeds and ensuring that the plants had water enough to keep them growing.

As she climbed steadily upward, Andhra realized that the effort entailed in pram pushing was considerable. She had to slow her pace to a crawl to avoid breaking out in heavy perspiration. But Sanjay loved this unaccustomed movement and strange scene. He lay entranced, staring at the green palms and blue sky glimpsed from below the canopy. For that the effort was worthwhile.

Near the far edge of the estate, the workers' huts began. Andhra was glad she need not run the gauntlet of walking between them to be stared at, for the path to Robert's bungalow turned off the opposite way, giving him some privacy.

He was sitting in a cane chair on the veranda, flanked by pots of flowering plants. His injured leg rested on a footstool, and his crutches were propped beside him.

"Please don't get up," she called from the foot of the steps, but at the sight of her, he scrambled to his feet, his face transformed with astonished pleasure.

"This is magic! I was feeling thoroughly bored and frustrated, and then *you* suddenly appear," he exclaimed.

She made the pram safe and climbed the steps.

"I wanted to see for myself how you were progressing. I would have come earlier but—"

She broke off, gazing critically at him. "You look well. It appears that your bearer is taking more care of you than I'd feared."

"And you look a picture. God, I'd almost forgotten how beautiful you are!"

"I'll pretend I didn't hear that. If you make things difficult I'll regret coming."

"Sorry, I got carried away. Do sit down and I'll find you a drink." He pulled forward another cane chair and limped inside.

"My bearer has gone shopping," he explained when he reappeared with two glasses of pineapple juice. "We manage to tolerate each other reasonably well. My main grouse has been boredom through inactivity, but I mean to change that from now on. I've progressed to the stage where I can manage my crutches, so I'll get out increasingly from now on and take up the reins again on the estate. I don't fully trust Shukur Thayar to carry out my orders."

"Neither does Ranjana, but everything looked under control as I passed through the plantation. He's visiting the Cochpur Palace this afternoon. He couldn't very well escape it, it being Satish's birthday, but I made the excuse that I had to relieve Mumtaz with the baby."

"So it's to Satish that I owe this welcome sight of you," he said shrewdly. "I never liked him or his father, but they have their uses."

She laughed. The sound was like a tinkling fountain. Her beautifully sculptured face was alight with animation, because it was such a refreshing change to talk again to this man with his Western viewpoint after being swamped with smothering Eastern taboos at the palace.

A shadow fell across the veranda, and there stood Shukur

Thayar, gazing on them from the lower step with his basilistic stare.

"I saw the carriage of the *chota sahib* and wondered if Prince Ranjana was here," he said smoothly.

"He is not, so you can go back to your duties," Robert said coldly. "Tomorrow I shall venture out to see for myself what progress is being made."

"You will find all well, sahib." With a sly glance at Andhra, the Tamil turned away.

"Now it will be all over the palace that we've been having a tête-à-tête at my bungalow," he said savagely when they were alone.

She clenched her hands. "Don't worry. I, of course, would have mentioned the visit to my husband in any case. There's no reason at all to conceal it."

Except that he had expressly warned her not to lay herself open to unfavorable comments by going alone to the manager's bungalow, she reflected uneasily. And being a prince, Ranjana expected his commands to be obeyed, even by his wife.

"I should hate to be the cause of dissension between two such valued friends," Robert said slowly. "Much as I've longed for a glimpse of you and appreciate your presence now, I think it would be better not to come again. In any case, as the improvement in my leg continues, I shall be coming to the palace frequently to discuss things with Ranjana. I must be content with seeing you then."

At this tacit admission of his latent regard for her, Andhra realized how unwise she had been to take Ranjana's words so lightly. From now on she must tread warily for the sake of all three of them.

She stayed awhile longer but the earlier rapport was gone, and there was constraint between them when they parted.

The return, being downhill, was very much easier. She would have enjoyed the walk, with the bell birds calling in the tall trees and gaudy butterflies flitting across her path, but for the nagging unease that lay at the back of her mind. Telling Ranjana would not be easy.

She was spared the ordeal, for that evening at least. He was very late coming back, and she was in bed and falling asleep when she had a vague impression of the connecting door between their rooms opening, his glancing in on her, then quietly withdrawing as though loath to wake her.

The following morning he rose early. She heard him splashing about in the bathroom and talking to his servant Jaykar; then all was silent. He had no doubt gone out for a brief before-breakfast horseback ride on the estate, something he had begun to do now the later hours were becoming uncomfortably hot.

She rose, took her own bath, then went to the nursery to see little Sanjay. He had slept better last night, Mumtaz assured her with a smile. Evidently the unaccustomed outing had done him some good.

She had just returned to her room and was preparing to go down to breakfast when the door was thrust open with some violence, and Ranjana stood there looking uncommonly angry.

"So you see fit to disregard my wishes and lay yourself—and me, too—open to humiliation!" he exclaimed through set teeth.

Her heart seemed to turn over. That vile deposed manager had lost no time in spreading the salacious tidbit around. Innocuous though the brief call had been, Shukur Thayar would undoubtedly have given it a sly twist and reveled in the process.

Anguish kept her dumb. Ranjana had never before displayed such anger toward her. She felt she could not bear it.

"I expressly warned you of the consequences of calling alone on Robert Pearson," Ranjana went on. "You'd never get five yards, let alone up to his bungalow, without being seen and speculation aroused. I thought you had a greater sense of responsibility than to sully your name, particularly as we are not yet fully accepted here. It is merely playing into Uncle Balbir's hands."

"I'm sorry about that, but it seems intolerable if one cannot pay a friendly call on a sick person without the wrong interpretation being put on it," she said heatedly. "That sly creature Shukur Thayar must go. He's obviously hand and glove in with your uncle and a source of trouble."

"He also happens to be well in with the estate workers and able to sway their opinion. It would cause more trouble if I dismissed him just when the young tea plants are at a critical stage and need constant care. Losing Robert Pearson would be preferable, I think. There are experienced tea-plantation managers in Ceylon. No doubt I could find one ready enough to come here at the right salary."

She stared in dismay. "How can you talk so after he saved you from injury, if not death? Where is your sense of gratitude?"

"My dear Andhra, that was merely a trick of fate. He happened to lean forward at the crucial second and so caught what was intended for me. Of course I feel indebted to him, and I liked him in the first place. Now, since you've made so public your own liking, I'm not so keen. I don't intend to stand by and let you throw away everything on a man of another race and color. Until I decide what to do, you'll not go near him again."

Now she was on her mettle. Her dark eyes flashed in rebellion. "I never thought to hear you talk like your uncle Balbir, as though you owned me body and soul. I don't intend to live in purdah for the rest of my life just because I married a prince!"

Now it was his eyes that flashed fire in lightning response. "Take care, my pearl. You already have far more privileges and freedom than others of your status. Don't forget I'm entitled to take another wife if I'm so inclined, or as many concubines as take my fancy. Rakhee the dancing girl would be overjoyed to start the ball rolling."

It was absolutely true, but that did not lessen her sense of outrage. Dumb with shock, she stood staring until he turned away with an imperious, "Breakfast is waiting. Come, we don't want to give the servants any further cause for talk."

Damn the servants, and damn Ranjana for spoiling what had promised to be a beautiful day, she reflected as she followed him down. Never before had he acted toward her like the all-powerful prince he undoubtedly was. Hurt beyond measure, she retired into her shell and spoke only in answer over breakfast.

For the rest of the day, she was tense and unhappy, and it was a relief that she saw Ranjana only at meals. In their state of constraint, he had not mentioned how the events of the previous day had gone. Doubtless the celebrations had included dancing girls, with Rakhee figuring prominently among them. Doubtless Ranjana, along with the other men, had sat entranced as she postured before them in her flimsy draperies. Was he still thinking of her, aroused by the sultry promise of her voluptuous display?

With such thoughts tormenting her all day, Andhra worked herself into a state that ended with a sick headache. She went to bed early and for the first time in her married life turned the key in the lock of the door between their bedrooms.

It was a long time afterward, just as she was drowsing off into sleep, that the handle of the door turned. She did not hear that slight sound, only the result when Ranjana found himself actually barred from her.

A furious knocking followed, and his voice demanding to be let in.

"I have a headache and can't see you tonight," she called back, still sensitively shrinking from the thought of his touching her with this shadow between them.

"How dare you bar me! If you don't unlock the door this minute, I'll burst the lock!"

The savagery of his tone set her shivering, but she still could not bring herself to let him into her bed in the usual joyous fashion and act as though they were in rapport and no harsh threats had been flung her way in anger.

There was a long drawn out moment of silence while he found some tool to aid him, and then a sharp blow on the lock that shattered the old, flimsy structure.

The door was flung open. He stood there, looming larger than life in the dim lamplight, breathing heavily from anger and exertion. Even in this extremity, she thrilled to the sight of his bronze torso, as virile as a Greek god's, while quailing at the savage gleam in his eye and the flash of his white teeth in an almost tigerish smile.

"So! It has come to this—that I must rape my own wife!"

His low tone set her shuddering with mingled apprehension and fear. "I have a headache. I just want to be left alone tonight," she murmured unevenly.

"A convenient excuse, my pearl. You are no longer your own mistress to decide when I may or may not make love to you, but Princess Andhra, my wife, remember?"

So saying, he flung off the cotton wrap from his waist, jerked off the single sheet that covered her and fell upon her in a fury.

No gentleness tonight. For the first time his roughness caused her physical pain. She cried out in protest but he showed no mercy until, fired by his burning desire, her own emotions raced away from her will and made her his willing, pliable slave.

Fused together, they lay at last spent and silent until his kiss, gentle and contrite now on her bruised and bleeding lips, asked her forgiveness.

She gave it freely, happy that the rift between them was healed. He was her shining prince again, and she his proud and loving princess.

CHAPTER SIX

The heat grew more sultry every day, and with it the strange tension that hung over the estate. Under Robert Pearson's charge again, the tea plants thrived. All the coolies were re-housed, and the estate took on a neat and well-kept air, in sharp contrast to the rundown appearance it had presented when Ranjana and Andhra took over, with its dilapidated shacks and untidy plots.

Yet underneath was an air of sullen discontent. Someone was undoubtedly casting a wrench in the works, and there seemed little doubt that this was Shukur Thayar, acting under the instructions of Balbir, whom he went to see often.

"What's the matter with the stupid coolies!" Andhra exploded one morning to Mumtaz. "Can't they realize how much better off they are going to be from now on, with constant employment, care if they become sick, and a school and hospital soon to be built on the estate for their exclusive use. Surely they don't hanker after the old haphazard life, with constant fear of drought and famine, and disease striking down so many."

Mumtaz looked troubled. "Strange as it may seem, my princess, many of them do. They are so superstitious, and lived by fate before you came. If they starved or were afflicted, the gods decreed it and they meekly submitted. Now they are afraid that with all these unnatural changes, as they see them, Lord Siva will be angry and send worse afflictions to bedevil them. Besides—" She stopped short, obviously reluctant to say more.

"Pray continue," Andhra urged. "You are my only true friend here, and I look on you more as a friend than a servant. Yet mixing among the servants, you are bound to hear things. What are they saying about Ranjana and me?"

"There *are* whispers and rumors," Mumtaz went on unwillingly. "That Prince Ranjana is a usurper and has no right here. That he married a girl of low caste picked from the gutter as a child by an English officer and brought up in outlandish Western fashion. That your son is not of true royal blood and will not be fit to rule over them when his turn comes. Also . . ."

"Go on, my dear Mumtaz."

"The whispers go that your morals are corrupt and you have a secret liaison with Robert Pearson. They say that is why you brought him from far Darjeeling and set him in the place of Shukur Thayar."

Andhra clenched her hands in impotent anger. She felt sick with humiliation for both herself and Ranjana.

Mumtaz laid a gentle hand on her shoulder. "Do not be angry, my princess. Mumtaz knows that all these suspicions are false. She also knows the source of them, for without doubt that scheming Balbir Mukti is behind these insinuations and paying Shukur Thayar to spread them. He would dearly love to make life so difficult for you both that you would be glad to go and leave the estate to him, the true owner, as he sees it."

Andhra nodded. Her own conclusion exactly, though she had not realized feelings were running so high against her. What if some form of sabotage should break out and the young tea plants be deliberately ruined? How cruel a blow that would be for Ranjana. Had he been perceptively right when he had threatened to dismiss Robert?

Her hackles rose at the mere thought. He was a splendid organizer, and it would be quite unjust to get rid of him. Robert was entirely without blame, for although she knew he secretly loved her, he had never overstepped the mark in any way and was the most loyal of men.

"I'll talk over these things with Ranjana," she said slowly. "Something must be done. Now try sponging little Sanjay down with cool water and see if that stops his fretful cries. The heat tries him even more than it does us, I'm afraid."

"Also the *chota sahib* is teething," Mumtaz said with a sigh. "He is truly to be pitied, poor sweeting."

Andhra went straight to Ranjana to pass on all that Mumtaz

had confided. He was naturally angry and upset, especially at the slur cast on Andhra's rank and upbringing.

"It matters little," she soothed him, "so long as *you* are happy with me and my ancestry. Father never spoke of my origins, preferring to regard me as his own daughter, except once when I showed curiosity and he told me to remember only that my natural father was of high status and my caste impeccable. What worries me most is this vile insinuation about Robert and me. You suspected it earlier when you considered dismissing him, but I feel that would be most unjust. Even from the most mercenary angle, you would never find a better manager."

"I know it, and yet. . . ."

"The answer," she said slowly, "might be for me to go away for a while. That should prove there is nothing save friendship between Robert and me and might go a long way toward restoring harmony with the coolies."

He stared. "Where would you go, my pearl?"

"Why, up to Darjeeling, of course, to visit Jenny. She urged me to come when the heat became oppressive down here in the south. I would take Mumtaz and Sanjay, of course. The bracing mountain air would do him a world of good. He's been fretful and off his food, as you know, since the hot weather coincided with cutting his first teeth, poor mite."

Ranjana began to pace up and down, troubled by mixed emotions.

"It would certainly do you both good, for your health," he said at last, "and with the splendid new railway between Madras and Calcutta, the journey would be quite tolerable. But by all the gods, how could I bear the parting?"

She went close and put her hands on his shoulders. "If it would be too painful for you, I'll forget all about it, my prince."

"No, no, I cannot be so selfish. Besides, as you say, the move might help to settle the rumors on the estate. It would not be for long. Two months or so, shall we say. Surely I can manage without you for so short a time, when we have a lifetime to spend together."

"I shall miss you just as much and long for the day I see you again." She sighed. "But we must think of little Sanjay, apart from these other matters."

So very soon Andhra, Mumtaz and the baby found themselves in the great, noisy station at Madras, where hissing steam engines came and went like fearful dragons, pulling a snakelike line of coaches behind. Here on the platforms families camped out for days and nights waiting for trains, equipped with bedding rolls, stoves and kettles, bundles of clothes and baskets of food.

Andhra was more fortunate. A first-class sleeping compartment with every comfort they could think of had been reserved for her party, and they took possession of it a short while before the train was due to begin its long journey north.

Ranjana waited to wave them off. There were tears in Andhra's eyes when she drew her head through the open carriage window, leaving him only a blur in the distance. This was their first parting since their marriage. Would he miss her too badly? What if loneliness should force him to turn to the willing charms of Rakhee? The thought was devastating.

But soon the passing scenery drove away such unwelcome visions. The beaten earth road running parallel to the rail track was deeply rutted and parched with drought. Every lumbering ox cart creaking along sent up clouds of dust that enveloped the patient coolies trudging behind. Life was difficult for the poor in India, whatever the season.

This also applied to train travel. While Andhra rolled along in spacious privacy, the masses were in a sorrier plight. Packed tightly to the point of suffocation in every third-class carriage, they were denied a clear view and even free access to the dust-laden air because of the hangers-on outside filching a free ride. These nimble-footed urchins had leaped up to the carriage steps while the train chugged slowly out of the station, before it gathered speed, and clung to any hold, regardless of smut, smoke, or the danger of losing their grip. As fast as they vacated their precarious positions on reaching a station, others took their place.

While the train was actually at rest in the stations, vendors of food, drink and many other commodities moved in, thrusting their wares up at the sea of faces peering from the yawning windows. Andhra firmly refused all these offers, noting with a shudder the flies clustering on the sticky sweetmeats and the mounds of dusty rice. Small wonder that epidemics were rife and disease cut short so many lives.

She did not care to trust the drinks, either. With a stock of tea and a kettle, they were quite independent. At every stop Mumtaz would race down the platform to the engine and have the kettle filled with boiling water. Even without milk, the tea was refreshing and kept them going, with the food they carried, for the whole of the three-day journey.

Each evening the upper bunks were let down and, with the addition of their own bedrolls, made tolerable beds for the night, though sleep was spasmodic.

"The *chota sahib* has stood the journey very well," Mumtaz declared, beaming at her charge as they stepped down at Howrah Station on the south bank of the Hooghly River.

They crossed by ferry boat to Calcutta, where Andhra had a joyous meeting with Jenny. Here they spent a day seeing the sights and exercising their cramped limbs before pushing on in a steamboat up a sluggish river that flowed between great spreads of paddy fields, golden vistas of mustard flowers and towering bamboo clumps.

"What a blessing it will be for you when the railroad is finally laid right up to Darjeeling," Andhra said. "You are so cut off at the moment."

"True, and the final part of the track is going to be fiendishly difficult to build over such a steep ascent," her adoptive sister agreed. "But Mark loves challenge and is getting tremendous satisfaction out of planning it all. Besides, Darjeeling is so lovely neither of us would want to live anywhere else."

She was right, Andhra agreed, when two horse-drawn gharries finally pulled them and their luggage into the spectacular hill station nestling beneath the towering, snow-capped Himalayas. Having been built mostly by the British, there were no spectacular temples like those that were taken for granted in most parts of India, but the breathtaking panoramas on every hand more than made up for the lack. Neat bungalows and well-kept gardens full of flowers, flanked by the bright green of flourishing tea estates, largely made up the small town, and in one of these bungalows lived Jenny and Mark.

"How lucky you are to have no water problem," Andhra declared, gazing at the roses and hollyhocks with appreciation. "Down in the south we're now in a state of drought. But for the constant attention of garden boys, our lawns would be burned to cinders."

Jenny laughed. "We get too much rain at times, but one can't have it all ways."

Mark greeted Andhra in the warmest fashion. How good it was to see his rugged English face again. He seemed particularly taken with little Sanjay, and she had the distinct impression that he longed for a son of his own. What a pity that they were still childless, for Jenny, too, could not conceal her yearning whenever she looked at Andhra's perfect princeling.

Life settled into a peaceful groove. Sanjay lost his fretfulness and thrived in the invigorating hill air. Andhra walked, rode or went shooting with Mark and almost felt herself back in her premarriage days when she, Jenny and their father had lived in the same fashion, until the mutiny.

But after the first fortnight, when the novelty had worn thin, Andhra found her thoughts returning more and more to the Summer Palace, so far away, and to Ranjana, her prince. Did he miss her as fervently as she was beginning to miss him? How did he spend his time when he was not occupied by the estate, now that he no longer had her and Sanjay to absorb him. Did he perhaps go more frequently to Cochpur in search of diversion, to eat in the exclusive restaurants and thrill to the sultry delights of the dancing girls? Especially Rakhee?

By the end of the first month, she was so restless that Jenny could not fail to notice. "You're missing Ranjana, which of course is natural. What a pity he could not come, too, for a few weeks," she said at breakfast one morning.

"Oh, he'd never leave the estate for any length of time. Not yet, until things are running absolutely smoothly," Andhra said. "It means such a lot to him. Perhaps I ought to return now. I've been away long enough to silence malicious tongues."

"But it's doing little Sanjay so much good here. At least stay until the hottest weather passes," Jenny demurred, obviously loath to part with the baby.

Suddenly Andhra's mind was made up. "He shall stay with you for a while longer, but I'll start back tomorrow. With Mumtaz and you to dote on him, he won't miss me. Later I'll coax Ranjana to come up on a brief visit with me to fetch Sanjay home. What do you say to that?"

"A good plan, Andhra dear. If I can't have you both, I'll settle for Sanjay." Jenny laughed.

"I've just remembered something I'm certain you'll be interested to see," Jenny said that afternoon while they were relaxing on the veranda. "It's a letter from our old ayah. Do you remember how she left suddenly to go to her daughter who was sick? It was just before the mutiny broke, and we never saw her again."

"Why of course I remember. How is she?"

"Still near the same village. I'll bring the letter and you can read it for yourself."

"She must have asked someone to write it for her," Andhra said when Jenny reappeared, "being quite illiterate."

"Yes, the British nun in the mission hospital where she now lives. Ayah is very frail, I gather, but she helps out to the best of her ability with the children who were orphaned by the mutiny."

Andhra took the letter and read with great interest the few lines in small neat script. Apparently an old newspaper had found its way into the convent, carrying the story of the proposed spectacular railway to be built right up to Darjeeling, chiefly to aid the quality tea trade. As the engineer in charge, Mark's photograph had figured in the account, together with a picture of Jenny, bringing the past vividly back to their ayah's fading memory. She had induced one of the kindly nuns to write, inquiring how her favorite, Andhra, was faring these days.

"Not knowing our precise address, the letter was simply addressed to Chief Engineer Mark Copeland, Darjeeling," Jenny explained. "But he's so well known that it found us without difficulty. I wrote back telling her of your marriage and exalted status. She'll be very proud to know you're now a princess and the mother of a baby son."

Andhra smiled at the thought. "I'll jot down the address of the convent and write to her myself on my return to Cochpur," she declared. "A present for her and a donation to the nuns would be welcome, I guess."

"I had the same thought," Jenny agreed. "I sent a parcel of our best tea and a hundred rupees along. There are always so many mouths to feed at these places. The poorest coolies dump unwanted girl babies by the dozen on their doorstep in times of flood and drought."

It was a wrench to say good-bye to Jenny and more especially to her enchanting, dimpled baby, but it would be only for a short time, Andhra consoled herself. In a matter of weeks she would be back, hopefully with Ranjana, to collect their treasure. The worst of the heat should be over then, and the Summer Palace at Cochpur a pleasant place again.

It was only when she was seated in the train on the tedious journey back that she realized the imminence of her husband's birthday and that she would just about make it home in time. Would he feel obliged to celebrate it in the manner customary among the highborn in India? If so, she could arrive to a house full of his uncongenial relatives. The thought was galling in the extreme and took away much of her burning anticipation. She had wanted to surprise him by turning up out of the blue, and her blood had raced hotly through her veins as she imagined the passionate reunion. Now the reality might not be all joy.

The journey, without Mumtaz and the baby to distract her, seemed longer, but at last the train pulled into the teeming Central Station and she climbed down and threaded her way between the bundles, boxes and babies of the families squatting all around.

The disadvantage of returning unexpectedly was that no one waited to meet her with the essential carriage. However, a whole string of vehicles from ox carts to horse gharries waited hopefully outside the impressive building for a fare that would provide the next meal of rice. Ignoring the importuning cries of the rickshaw coolies, Andhra picked out the most robust-looking horse and was assisted into a creaking gharry by its jubilant driver.

It was now late morning, so it would be near dark before they reached the Summer Palace on the hill slopes. But there was still a little food and water remaining in the basket Jenny had provided for her long journey. Andhra settled back on the worn seat with resignation as the driver climbed up and they swung out into the bustle of Victorian Madras.

After the peace of Darjeeling, set like a jewel amid the tea estates beneath the mighty Himalayas, Madras seemed claustrophobically crowded. With consummate skill the driver guided his vehicle through a maze of rickshaws, bullock carts, horse gharries and pedestrians, all milling around commodities of every kind spilling out from the dark little shops lining the streets. Sacred cows meandered at will, a further hazard to progress, and mangy dogs slinked among the debris piled in corners.

It was a relief to leave the city behind and gain the quiet of the beaten-earth country roads. Yet even here conditions were far from perfect. Clouds of dust rose from the parched earth and enveloped them at every overloaded ox team they passed, churned up by the heavy wooden wheels of the carts and the lumbering hooves of the beasts of burden. Andhra drew her gauzy scarf close about her head and face and gave thanks that at least the shabby awning of the gharry protected her from the burning rays of the sun, now beating down from a brassy sky.

The relief of the rainy season was a long way off, yet the sultry heat suggested a brewing storm. They did develop occasionally out of the blue, especially in the hill regions of southern India, subject as it was to the influence of both southwest and northeast monsoons. But Andhra hoped it would not break before she reached the comfort of home.

Hours later she was there at last. She paid off the hired vehicle and walked eagerly across the bridge spanning the lake. All fatigue fell away with the realization that within minutes she would be back with her prince, folded in his embrace, and that tonight they would sleep together again, close in body and spirit, drowsy with sweet fulfillment.

The brief dusk of the tropics had now fallen. The palace gardens on either side of the short drive were hushed and heavy with the scent of blossom stealing out like incense. A rush of nostalgia caught at her throat at the familiar beauty of it all.

And then on the drive ahead she saw them—Ranjana and Rakhee the dancer—walking close together, oblivious of anyone save themselves.

Shocked surprise halted Andhra in her eager surge forward. What was he saying to her to bring that tinkling laugh and turn her alluring face up to his? How long had they been together out here?

Had it been a mistake to go off to Darjeeling and leave Ranjana alone? Had he been driven to the arms of one who was all too ready and willing to console him?

CHAPTER SEVEN

Although she was not conscious of it, some small sound of dismay must have escaped Andhra as she stood staring ahead, for the two figures halted abruptly and turned to face her. Rakhee, adept at sly diplomacy, glided away when she realized the situation, leaving Ranjana to deal with it.

"Andhra, my pearl, you are the last person I expected to see," he said, moving toward her. "Why have you returned so suddenly without letting me know? I would have sent transport to meet you."

"It appears to be high time I did return." Her voice was stiff with constraint, and she turned her face so that his mouth just brushed her cheek instead of reaching her lips.

He frowned. "Don't be absurd, my love. Uncle Balbir and his family are here for the evening. It happens to be my birthday, remember, so they are returning the compliment I paid them when I joined their celebrations for Satish's birthday awhile back. They brought along a few entertainers from Cochpur town, among them Rakhee."

"Then why isn't she entertaining them instead of strolling out here with you?"

"Must you cross-examine me like a common thief!" A touch of asperity had crept into his tone. "Rakhee was hot after her efforts this sultry evening and slipped out for some air. I simply wanted to escape from the inane chatter of Balbir's wife and her cronies. I left them gorging on sweetmeats. However, I'd better get back before I'm missed. And you, my love, will be glad of some refreshment, I'm sure. But where are Mumtaz and Sanjay? I thought the mountain air was doing you all so much good it would be difficult to drag you away."

"I've left them there for a while. I missed you so much I

couldn't stay away any longer," she said slowly. "You apparently found consolation easily enough."

He grasped her shoulders, his fingers biting deep. "Don't turn a mild flirtation into something ugly, Andhra. I've given you no cause for complaint yet."

She thought of her own innocent friendship with Robert Pearson. That had not been viewed in a tolerant light by Ranjana or anyone else on the estate. It was intolerable to have one law for the husband and another for the wife, as in rural India. But this was no time to make a scene, with Balbir and his clan here, ready to blow up every incident and turn it to their own use. So she only said flatly, "We'd better go in. How are estate matters since my absence?"

"Reasonably smooth." He took her hand as they turned toward the palace, but her fingers lay unresponsive in his. "Pearson is fully recovered and in charge again, and the young tea plants are developing well. Next year we should be able to start plucking from the larger cuttings, but the seedlings will take up to three years."

They made for the large open courtyard where, in consideration of the sultry heat, the feasting and entertainment were being held. Ranjana thrust Andhra forward with a laughing, "See what an affectionate wife I have. Even the charms of the cool Himalayas could not hold her when my birthday drew near. She has journeyed all that way alone to join the celebrations."

Madhumita and her cronies murmured greetings and pressed refreshments upon her. Balbir and his son Satish just stared with black, expressionless eyes. They were not glad to see her back. They would far rather have had Ranjana join her in faraway Darjeeling, never to return. Their envy and hatred were as potent as ever, she realized somberly as she sank down on a low divan while Ranjana walked among his guests, making sure that they lacked for nothing.

Across the open center expanse where a sitar player strummed a soulful accompaniment to the monotonous singing of his partner, Andhra caught sight of Robert Pearson. He stood near some potted palms, looking bored and a trifle cynical. No doubt he realized as well as she the undercurrent of jealousy and hatred masked by this false show of amiability, and that Uncle Balbir and his family would never change unless and until they finally filched this estate for themselves.

Meeting her eye, he shrugged expressive shoulders and smiled wryly. No doubt he was as surprised as Ranjana at her unexpected return, but he had not sought her out to discover the reason or even say hello. Wisely, perhaps, with the eyes and ears of this family upon them.

The singing ended at last, and a band of instrumentalists took the space to produce a rousing crescendo of sound while a male dancer leaped and contorted in a frenzy of fervor. Madhumita, sprawling beside Andhra among the cushions, smiled and clapped her approval, then reached greedily for more sticky sweetmeats from the low table in front of her to stuff into her pudgy cheeks.

Andhra glanced away, feeling slightly sick. The sultry heat and the long ride over bumpy roads had produced the beginning of a headache. All she wanted now was peace and quiet—any refuge from this garish scene.

Surely there was no overwhelming reason for her presence. The party had begun without her and could quite well finish without her. Since they would undoubtedly be staying here for the night, she would not be expected to say good-bye until morning.

So while Madhumita laughed until she almost choked on a nut at the antics of the dancer, Andhra quietly rose and slipped away.

Beyond the bright circle of lanterns illuminating the courtyard, the garden stretched silent and inviting. A great yellow moon above made it almost as bright as day, casting shadows of shrubs and palm trees in sharp relief. Night birds called, and the perfume of tobacco plants stole out like incense.

It was irresistible. She moved swiftly out onto the drive and walked toward the bridge spanning the shimmering water of the lake and the estate. This gained, she paused, leaning on the bamboo handrail and staring out across the lake. How beautiful it was.

"So you've no more stomach for sham cordiality than I have?"

She glanced up. It was Robert Pearson, standing beside her, his pipe sending an agreeable aroma to join the other night scents.

"I badly needed a smoke to offset that lot," he said as though to excuse his presence.

She smiled wryly at him. "No doubt, but you weren't very diplomatic to follow me out. You know what suspicious minds some of them have."

He sighed. "You're quite right, but I was on the point of leaving in any case, so it was pure chance really that you happened to walk this way, my way home. Needless to say, it's a great joy to have you around again, but I hope nothing serious brought you back so unexpectedly."

"Not really. I just happened to want Ranjana too badly to stay away any longer," she said candidly.

His hands clenched on the bamboo rail close to her own, showing how acutely he felt the situation.

"He must be delighted to have you back," he said at last.

"Maybe, but men so easily find consolation denied to women in this country. I find some of the traditions hard to bear and noticed the difference in Darjeeling, living with Jenny and Mark, in a largely British community. That's why it is so comforting to have you on the estate. Though I'm Indian by birth, my largely European upbringing allowed too much emancipation for me to fit very easily into a Hindu niche, I'm afraid. I don't quite belong."

Turning her head to glance up at him, she noticed a shadow back on the drive that quickly vanished to merge with the ornamental shrubs lining it. A trick of the moonlight, no doubt.

The next moment the moon was blotted out as an inky cloud scudded ominously over it, threatening an out-of-season storm, and a vivid flash of lightning illuminated the scene instead.

"The storm's about to break at last. It's been threatening all day," he said hurriedly. "The parched estate needs it, but you'd better make a bolt for the palace before you get drenched."

"What about you? It's quite a way to your bungalow."

"I'll survive."

She glanced up as a deafening roar of thunder rent the air, to feel the splash of huge raindrops on her face and head. As always with tropical storms, its eventual eruption was swift and devastating.

"You'd better come back and take shelter. You'd be mad to walk back through this," she called, her sandaled feet speeding up the drive.

He caught up to her as she reached the arcade leading to the courtyard. Here they both halted abruptly, surprised by the sight of Ranjana, Uncle Balbir and Satish standing waiting like an inquisition. Behind them lurked Shukur Thayar, a half smile on his shifty face.

Immediately Andhra connected the shadow she had seen on the drive with him. He must have noticed her stealing away from the entertainment, followed by Robert. He had shadowed him to spy on them and hurried back to inform the entire gathering of their assignation, as he would term it.

Ranjana wore a black frown. "I was just about to come and fetch you back. Shame on you for stealing away from your guests, and with none other than Pearson. Your behavior is unpardonable."

Uncle Balbir's black eyes seemed to spit venom. "It is clear that the liaison between them is not over, in spite of the parting. You are being deceived and duped, my dear nephew. Your wife is not fit to reign here with you and be the mother of your sons. She is doubtless of low caste, and bad blood will out. You should put her away."

This was too much for Ranjana. He turned on Balbir, grasping the skinny shoulder. "I'm quite capable of dealing with my wife in the way I think fit, you old schemer. How dare you utter such remarks in public, since they bring disrepute on me and my son as well as Andhra. You will take them back at once and apologize to us both."

"Never, since they are obviously true," snarled the older man. "It is the greatest pity either of you ever came here from the north, to steal what should have been mine and bring unwanted change and shame to the family."

"My father is right," Satish declared, thrusting himself forward. "It was a black day for us all when you appeared with your outrageous plans that flout tradition. The coolies distrust you and your sweeping changes and fear that no good will come of it. You are an unwanted usurper and should go back to your north country before harm comes to you and yours." He spat venomously at Ranjana's feet.

At this insult Ranjana scowled blackly. No man could act so under his own roof and get away with it. His right fist, trained so well at college in England, shot out fair and square to the pugnacious chin and snarling mouth, meeting it with such impact that blood began to flow from a gaping split.

"Now get out, the lot of you!" he roared. "You are an affront to my eyes, and I never want to see you again!"

"But you will, my fine nephew." Balbir stepped to his son's side, mopping at his streaming mouth. "I swear you'll live to regret this, and ever setting foot in Cochpur. By all the gods, you'll be glad to leave before long, mark my words."

He and his son stalked off to gather their women and order their horses and carriages to be prepared at once, while Shukur Thayar made to slink after them.

"Come back!" Ranjana commanded Shukur Thayar. "I have more to say to you. Since you are patently in league with Balbir and his son, you can go with them. I don't ever want to see your face on the estate again."

If looks could have killed, Ranjana would have dropped dead. The deposed manager muttered some curse under his breath, then turned and followed the others.

There was a moment's pregnant silence while Ranjana stared somberly at Andhra and Robert Pearson.

"I will save you the trouble of dismissing me by offering my resignation," Robert said at last. "But first let me assure you that neither Andhra nor I had any intention of an assignation. I simply went out to smoke my pipe, knowing it would not be tolerated in the courtyard. I happened to see Andhra on the bridge and went to speak to her."

"Absolutely true," Andhra agreed. "After a long day of travel, and with the heavy storm atmosphere hanging around, my head was beginning to ache. I just had to escape for a few minutes from Madhumita and her cronies. I was as much surprised by Robert's appearance as he was to see me."

"I believe you both," Ranjana said at last, "but that only

applies to me. The vile accusations spread by Balbir and his toadies will unfortunately be believed by everyone else. He made my advent here difficult enough, and no doubt things will now be even worse."

"That's all the more reason for retaining Robert, who is loyal, besides knowing so much about tea growing," Andhra said feelingly. "You can't let him go, Ranjana."

He shrugged his splendid shoulders. "We'll leave it until tomorrow and discuss it then, shall we? I feel quite fed up with everything at the moment, as the British so succinctly put it."

The storm was passing with the abruptness with which it had arrived. The rumbles of thunder were much farther off, and the lightning flickered less intensely. The deluge of rain had passed with it, and the moon shone again from a clearing sky.

Robert said good night and set off on the walk to his bungalow, leaving Andhra and Ranjana alone except for the servants clearing up in the courtyard.

"Come," he murmured, drawing her out into the garden. "Perhaps the peace and quiet outside will calm us both. You were piqued to see me with Rakhee earlier, while I in turn was jealous of Robert when that toad Thayar rushed in to say you were together. No doubt it is our intense love for each other that makes us so vulnerable. Now we will put it all behind us."

They kept to the paths, strolling hand in hand under the great yellow moon. The scents of the flowers were even more potent after the rain, and secret night life stirred around them.

They paused at the tiny temple in a far corner. Andhra rang the tinkling bell and prayed that their enemies might be confounded and Ranjana left to carry out his plans in peace.

"Now I feel happier, and ready to go in," she murmured.

"I, too. Ready to love you again. It is so long since we lay together, your divine body close to mine, my pearl."

His voice was hoarse and urgent. Encircling her with passionate arms, he drew her away from the temple, back to the now-quiet palace and the privacy of their own apartment.

CHAPTER EIGHT

It was nice to be home again with Ranjana at the Summer Palace, yet life had a strange, distinctly menacing quality. Andhra missed little Sanjay and Mumtaz very much, especially as Ranjana was out and about on the estate most of the time, helping Robert to plan and supervise the growing plantation.

Since the open rupture of relations between Ranjana and Balbir's family, there had been a noticeable lessening of cooperation from the coolies and their families, now housed in their compact new dwellings. Small irritations multiplied daily, which could not all be attributed to ill fortune, so that Robert and Ranjana were afraid to relax their supervision for a moment.

Clearly the wicked uncle's influence still reached out to the Summer Palace, even though Shukur Thayar was no longer employed there. This baleful domination included the indoor servants, too. They were less ready to obey, tardy in appearing when summoned, lax in carrying out orders and less respectful than they had been at first.

Without Mumtaz to act as a go-between and smooth her way, Andhra felt the full force of this subversive revolt. The cook, Gulam, presented the greatest difficulty, especially as his position entitled him to a daily interview to discuss menus and food purchases. He dawdled far too much, gossiping with cronies in the markets; fiddled the accounts outrageously; and showed a scarcely veiled contempt when she ventured to remonstrate or question his figures. If she was not satisfied, he implied, she could dismiss him and find someone else.

This course of action, she knew quite clearly, would mean a mass walkout of half the rest of the staff, Gulam being the virtual head of the domestics, as was the custom. Without the help of Mumtaz, the task of engaging new staff was too daunting to be contemplated. So it appeared that there was no course at present save to put up with the irritations.

The climax came one day about a fortnight after Andhra's return from Darjeeling. Ranjana came in around one o'clock for lunch, looking tired and cross, and slumped down in one of the cane chairs in the dining room.

"Things grow worse daily," he said somberly. "The wretched coolies are still clearly under the influence of my scheming uncle, who is out to ruin me and force me away from here. He somehow manages to supply them with rupees for arrack, which so befuddles them that they don't carry out Robert's orders properly. This morning he found a whole bed of seedling tea plants wilted beyond recall. They had forgotten to water them, they said, but it could just as well have been deliberate sabotage. Apart from Robert, I can't trust one of them on the whole estate."

Andhra looked stricken. "I'm in exactly the same position with the indoor servants. Cook is almost insolent since your uncle cast such a slur on my origins. It's even more difficult now I haven't Mumtaz to help and act as a go-between. I do miss her, and little Sanjay, too."

"Then go and bring them home, beloved. I confess I miss my son a great deal, too."

"I was hoping you could have gone with me this time for a short break. The change would be so good for you after all the worry you've had recently." She sighed.

He shrugged impatiently. "Not a hope, my love. I dare not risk leaving the estate at present. Who knows what might happen in my absence.

"What's happened to lunch today?" he added when there was no sign of the bearer. "I want to get out again as quickly as possible."

His violent ringing of the hand bell brought the house bearer with boiled chicken and rice. But though the smell was appetizing, the eating was a disappointment. The bird proved stringy and tough, and the rice mushy.

"This is nothing but a bag of bones, yet Cook swore he'd bought a prime chicken and charged me accordingly," Andhra said crossly as Ranjana pushed away his half-full plate. "He imposes on me quite shamelessly and almost dares me to sack him."

They fared no better with the *custel brun*. Caramel custard had always been a favorite sweet of Andhra's, but today it tasted as though it had been concocted from curdled milk. They were glad of the bowl of mangoes and bananas to fill up the corners.

Deeply dispirited, Andhra sought the solace of the long cane chair on the shady veranda after Ranjana had left, and there she lay thinking deeply.

Since this contempt of her stemmed from the slur cast on her birth by Uncle Balbir, if only she could establish that she came of a good background, as her adoptive father had assured her, the attitude of the servants indoors at least should change. How could she find out the truth of her origin?

Suddenly she remembered her old ayah, now living in retreat with the good sisters of mercy who rescued and cared for destitute children abandoned by their parents. Since Ayah had always been there in the dak bungalow as far back as Andhra could recall, she must have been engaged around the time of Jenny's birth and so would have been in charge when she herself was adopted by the British major and his wife as a toddler and joined the household.

It was a pity the far past was so shadowy. All Andhra could remember was a closely packed community of women and children, all of her own coloring, where she had lived as part of the group. Suddenly the community was gone. She had been whisked away to a strange world of white people with alien ways, where she had been acutely unhappy until she had adapted to this new world.

Baby Jenny had helped, and of course there had been dear Ayah. Ayah who was always so kind and patient, but who persistently refused to answer probing questions regarding Andhra's origins and parentage, firmly declaring that her lips were sealed by an oath of silence.

But now that the old woman was nearing her end and it no longer mattered except to Andhra, surely she could be induced to break her silence, if only she could be contacted personally.

With a sudden surge of hope, Andhra remembered the address Jenny had passed on to her. She had meant to write to the old woman before this, sending some little gift and money for the orphans, but the difficulties of life at the palace without Mumtaz had driven it from her mind. Now she must do better than write. She would go personally and have a heart-to-heart talk.

Then Andhra's hopes plummeted. The mission school in which Ayah had found sanctuary was situated on the banks of the river Rajpur, about twenty miles from Chandipur, the garrison town where Major Hilton had been stationed and where Andhra had spent her early childhood since her adoption, until school in England had claimed her and Jenny. The area being so remote, Ranjana would never allow her to set out alone to find it.

Yet he dare not leave the estate himself in the present state of unrest to help her in her search, so what way out was there?

A little innocent deception seemed the only solution. He did not mind her traveling up to Darjeeling alone. Indeed he had himself urged her to go and bring Sanjay and Mumtaz home. The journey by train in a first-class carriage between Madras and Calcutta was easy enough. And from Calcutta there was a well-used route by river and other means up to Darjeeling that by now was quite familiar to her. She must let Ranjana believe she would go straight to Darjeeling, then make a detour from Calcutta.

It would take longer to finally reach home with Sanjay and Mumtaz, of course, but if she could establish proof that she came of a high-caste family, Ranjana would forgive the mild deception.

To make life smoother for him she would face a much more daunting task than the one ahead. Dear Lord, how she longed to help him instead of being the burden she now felt herself to be. The future seemed bleak unless they could establish themselves in a better light with these southern coolies, so tradition bound and misled by the scheming Balbir Mukti.

Her mind now made up, she packed saris and underclothes

in a bundle, ordered a basket of food and drink from the cook, and was all set to go first thing next morning by the time Ranjana arrived back for dinner.

"I shall miss you, beloved," he confessed as they lay together that night. "But soon you will return with our son. He will be some compensation for us both during these difficult times. My hope is that the coolies will come to realize the benefits we bring when the new hospital and school are completed in Cochpur town."

"So building has begun. How is it progressing?"

He sighed. "Badly. There are unaccountable delays and mishaps, which privately I can only attribute to the influence of that wretched uncle of mine. His determination to ruin me and send me packing is only equaled by my own determination to stay and weather the storm and emerge the victor. When flourishing tea plantations cover these hills and we have a force of prosperous, content workers, I shall feel I've played my small part in shaping a better India."

"I pray you'll succeed, my prince. I'm certain you will in the end, and I would do anything to help," she murmured.

"All I want at the moment is your love, my pearl, your beautiful body that drives me mad with desire." He turned to her with hungry mouth and seeking hands that moved softly over the secret places of her, driving her so ecstatically wild that she almost wept until his perfect golden form covered her own and they soared once again to the heights together.

"Say you'll never forget me and turn to Rakhee the dancing girl," she murmured when, passion spent, they lay tranquil. "Although I know it is your right if you so choose, I could never bear to share you with another woman. You must be mine alone, my prince of love."

"It shall be so always, my pearl. I promise. How could I forget you in the brief time you will be away?"

"Maybe it won't be so very brief," she said, thinking of the detour ahead of her. "Perhaps Jenny will persuade me to stay a few days with her. But you are so busy now on the estate that you won't have time to grow bored. And there's always Robert to talk to."

Yet it was a wrench to tear herself away early the following morning and set off alone. Only the belief that she would be helping to lift the cloud of misfortune that threatened to ruin their dream of turning the estate into a flourishing concern with well-paid, content coolies set her resolutely on the way to Madras and the beginning of her secret mission.

How providential that she had been able to reserve at such short notice a first-class compartment shared only with one other woman, she reflected as she threaded her way along the crowded platform. Families squatted everywhere, with the usual bundles, baskets, bedding rolls and babies, cooking, shaving, eating and sleeping with the detached unconcern unique to India. Were they waiting for trains today, tomorrow or next week? It hardly seemed to matter. The monster drawn up at the platform seemed already full to bursting, with twenty or more third- and fourth-class passengers packed like sardines in their comfortless carriages. It was a miracle that they survived the heat to reach their journey's end.

Reaching the few first-class carriages, she found the one with her own name on the notice fixed on the door, together with that of a Mrs. N. Bannerjee. Mrs. Bannerjee was already in occupation when Andhra climbed inside. She proved to be middle-aged, plump and smiling, and Andhra decided on the spot that a long journey with her would be less difficult than with many people.

And so it proved as they rolled steadily northward over plains that had been parched and burning until the rainy season had arrived to bring welcome relief. Now the rivers were swelling from mere trickles in stony beds to recognizable streams able to carry boat traffic again. In the wet rice paddies women worked bent double, planting the precious seedlings one by one while coolies and bullocks tilled the black earth with their age-old wooden plows.

Andhra and her companion talked, ate and slept their harmonious way in comfort undreamed of by the unfortunate third- and fourth-class passengers. Whenever they stopped at a big station, a tray of food and drink would be carried in to them by the guard, while the less fortunate coolies had to settle for the fly-blown offerings thrust toward them by station vendors. They were equally favored at night, having a spacious bunk each on which to unroll their bedding and sleep in peace and their own toilet compartment in which to freshen themselves next morning.

Arriving at Howrah station, Andhra promptly secured a passage on a river steamer sailing up the Hooghly the following morning to join the Ganges and travel northwest. What nostalgic memories gripped her as she found herself retracing the journey she had made some years previously while fleeing from the horrors of the mutiny with Jenny and their friends who were lucky enough to have escaped. Now the journey was in reverse. She was traveling upriver, back toward Chandipur and the garrison fort where they had faced siege, attack and death, and her adoptive father had sustained the wounds that led to his death in England.

Blinking back the moisture that sprang to her eyes, she was glad that she would not be forced to see again the place of so much horror. The tributary river up which they now sailed was some miles from the fort, and the mission school was situated on its banks in the countryside, so she had found out.

The lazy days on the river passed like a dream. Andhra felt calmed and strengthened by the time her steamer berthed at a sweltering little town and the captain informed her that he went no farther.

"Mission school farther along river." He gestured to the dusty track running along the brown mud banks of the river. "You can be walking there, or maybe beg a ride in a bullock cart."

In the humid atmosphere that felt like a Turkish bath, she decided that a bullock cart was preferable, so she wandered a short way past bamboo thickets and found a shady patch under a flame of the forest tree, its bright red petals lying like drops of blood on the ground. Here she sat to wait with all the patience of her race until help should come along.

In the sultry heat there was little activity on the sluggish water. *Dhobi wallahs,* pot washers, water carriers had all completed their tasks earlier and sought the shade of their hovels. Even the harsh-voiced birds and chattering monkeys were silent in the banyan trees.

Presently the creaking of cumbersome wheels warned her

that a vehicle of some sort approached. Looking up, she was glad to see a long, narrow ox cart piled high with various bales and bundles moving toward her from the direction of the town. She was even more pleased to note that a single man occupied the high driving seat instead of the more usual crush of humanity. There was room and to spare for her.

Andhra rose and gathered up her bundle. Not knowing what contingencies she might meet on this diversion, she had purposely dressed in the plainest of her saris without ostentatious jewelry, so she did not present too incongruous a spectacle standing there on the rough track begging a lift.

The driver obligingly halted. In passable Hindi she asked how far the mission school was and if he would give her a lift for as far as he went.

With a cheerful grin he reached a hand for her bundle. It transpired that he was actually bound for that very destination, taking supplies and stores for the nuns.

So, with Andhra perched beside him, they creaked their slow way along past banyan trees and elephant grass until a formidable outcrop of rock reached right down to the banks of the river to block their way.

"We must go around by the road," the driver said, turning his vehicle ponderously left to follow the track over stony and rising ground that jolted them unmercifully.

It was quite a diversion. It would have taken her ages to walk it, she reflected when presently the obstruction was passed and they lumbered slowly down the descending slope to join the riverbank again.

Then quite soon they were there. A thick hedge of bamboos encircled a roomy compound enclosing neat thatched huts. A swarm of children played noisily around the buildings, not naked, dirty or ragged as many of the coolie children were, but each sporting a clean cotton garment that showed the nuns' care.

The ox-cart driver halted at the wide-open gate and began to unload his stores. Andhra, her heart beating faster because now she had reached her goal and would see and talk with dear old Ayah again, walked eagerly toward the central structure that proved to be an office with a young nun seated behind a desk.

As briefly as possible Andhra explained that an old woman residing here had once been her ayah and she would very much like to see her again. "Her name is Indu," she finished.

The young nun looked grave. "You knew that she was ill?"

"She did say that she was in poor health in a letter dictated to my sister," Andhra faltered, suddenly afraid.

The other nodded. "I remember the letter. I wrote it for her. Come, I will take you in to her. She often spoke of those old days. It will make her happy to see you again and bring joy to her passing."

"Her passing?"

"She is dying, I'm afraid."

Sadness descended on Andhra as she followed the nun to a small, austere room holding a single charpoy. Here, propped by pillows, lay the pale, emaciated form of the old woman who had ministered so lovingly to her young charges.

"Ayah! My dear, dear Ayah!" Andhra sank to her knees at the bedside and took the frail hands in hers. "It is so good to see you again," she said, tears starting to her eyes because it was all too obvious that a little later would have been too late.

"And you, my precious one," Ayah whispered in a voice that already had the hollowness of death. "Let me look on you once again before the sight fades from these old eyes." She peered searchingly up at the sweet young face bent above her and lifted one shaking hand to touch the contours, as though to imprint them forever on her mind.

"More beautiful than ever." The voice was a mere sigh as the hand fell weakly to the bed. "A true princess now, Jenny said, since you married the prince. Just as the gods destined for you, born a princess, my perfect one."

Andhra's heart almost stopped beating at this astounding revelation. Here was the answer to her prayers, the vindication of Ranjana's marriage to her and the destruction of Uncle Balbir, with his vile insinuations that threatened to wreck all their hopes and plans for the estate. But she must know more, must have some proof, if possible, for without it who would believe the word of a moribund old servant?

"A princess, Ayah? Now you must tell me more. It is quite vital," Andhra urged.

Ayah struggled to find words, but her voice was almost spent. At last, glancing at the nun hovering in the background, she managed to whisper, "Bring it, please. The treasure I carried next to my heart all these years."

The nun felt beneath the pillow and drew out a tiny pouch. "Had you not called in person today, I had instructions to send it to your sister in Darjeeling to pass on to you," she explained to Andhra as she placed the object in Ayah's clawlike hand.

Shakily the dying woman thrust it toward Andhra, whispering, "Take it, my precious. It is yours by right. You wore it when you first came to me, but my orders were to keep it hidden, like the truth of your birth. This I have done."

"But I must know more! Who were my parents, and why was I given away?" Andhra urged as gently as her eagerness allowed.

But the effort already made by the old woman, plus the excitement of seeing her young charge once more, had proved too much for the failing heart. As she took a long, sighing breath, her glazing eyes closed on the mortal world and life slipped away from the wrinkled face, leaving it gray and blank.

"She is gone," the nun said gently. "But her dearest wish was granted—to see you once again. Now she is at peace."

Andhra blinked back the tears as she followed the nun to her office. There she opened the tiny pouch and brought out a jeweled pendant. On a thin gold chain hung a tiny star composed of rubies and diamonds that twinkled and shone when the light struck them. There was no mistaking the quality of them.

"It's quite beautiful!" gasped Andhra. "Someone must have cared deeply for me to put such a treasure around my neck. Yet why should they give me away? Surely you can throw some light on it?"

The nun shook her head. "I know nothing except that you and Jenny were once in her charge, and that this pendant was to be given to you at her death. It seems probable that you were someone of high caste at birth, but why all the mystery, and why you should be adopted by a British officer and his wife, is beyond me. Now if you'll wait in here, I'll have a tray of tea sent in to you, and then I must go and make arrangements for Ayah's funeral."

She could do no good by staying for that, Andhra reflected as she sipped the fragrant brew. She still had a long journey before her to reach Darjeeling. It was better to set off immediately and discuss with Jenny the strange, dramatic disclosure of the past hour.

For a woman traveling alone, the pendant must be hidden from sight, she decided, fastening it around her neck and concealing it beneath the folds of her sari. Then she said good-bye to the kindly nun, left a generous gift of rupees for the orphans, and walked out of the compound gate on to the dusty, deserted road.

CHAPTER NINE

The delivery ox cart had unloaded and gone. Since it was too far to walk back to the river where she had disembarked from the boat in the heat, she sat down in some shade to wait for a likely-looking vehicle.

For an Indian road it was unusually quiet. Fifteen minutes passed before the familiar creaking heralded the usual mode of transport in rural parts. Andhra scrambled to her feet and picked up her bundle.

Instead of a sturdy cart with side slats like that which had transported her here, pulled by two hefty bullocks, a dilapidated contraption trundled into view. The cart was merely a few planks carrying bales of rice straw, pulled by one emaciated beast whose every bone thrust painfully from beneath the taut skin. Its driver was almost as dilapidated, with his ragged shift and unkempt appearance; he urged the weary beast on with a touch of the whip.

Andhra hesitated, loath to trust herself to such a conveyance, but her need decided the issue. It might be a long time before a better vehicle came along on this unfrequented track that seemed to lead nowhere.

The driver pulled up beside her. Was he bound for the town, she asked.

He was, and with the garrulous comradeship of India's poor, he offered his humble transportation as though it had been a maharaja's palanquin.

Seated among the bales, it was far from comfortable, creaking along on two great wooden wheels, jolted by every rut and stone on the atrocious track. Fortunately it would not be too long before she was able to get off and find a steamer due to sail for Calcutta or part of the way on which she could buy a passage. The rupees she had brought with her were safely hidden in an inner pocket and were sufficient to cover all expenses she might incur until she finally reached home again, accompanied by Mumtaz and baby Sanjay. A pang of longing went through her as she thought of his chubby face and great brown eyes.

Her pleasant reflections were brought to an abrupt end in mid-journey. With much effort on the part of the emaciated animal, and frequent applications of the whip, they had almost negotiated the ascent of the rising ground that blocked the way. Another five minutes and they would have safely reached the apex, veered around and taken the easy downward slope. But the stony, rutted track combined with the strain of the upward pull had proved too much for the aging coir ropes binding the cart shafts to the bullock. A final, excruciating jolt parted the fraying ropes abruptly, leaving the animal blessedly free of his burden and the cart careering backward down the slope they had just negotiated.

Pale with alarm, Andhra crouched among the bales until the rear end of the cart struck a huge boulder at the side of the track. It spun around, precipitating the driver straight at the boulder, along with most of the bales of straw, then continued its erratic way down, leaving Andhra alone in her dire peril.

Should she jump, she wondered wildly as the cart gathered speed, and risk breaking a limb, or hang on until some obstacle halted the headlong flight? The decision was made for her a few moments later. With no control to guide it, the cart ignored the slight deviation of the track, plunging straight forward right at the smooth gray trunk of a eucalyptus tree. Into this Andhra was flung as the cart disintegrated beneath her and fell in a useless heap.

Stunned, she lay bruised and unconscious, oblivious to everything under the oblique rays of the waning sun.

And so she was found some time later by a small group of strolling players who were tramping from a village beyond the mission school to the river town that had been Andhra's goal. But for the smashed cart they might easily have passed her by in the waning light, slumped as she was against the tree trunk.

As it was, they paused to investigate the cart in case anything of value should be lying around for the taking.

"Here is something," one of the two young men said in Hindi, holding up Andhra's bundle, dusty but intact.

"And here, too, my son!" Clacking her tongue, the old woman bent stiffly over the still form on the ground, feeling to see if the heart still beat.

"She lives. I think she is suffering from concussion, maybe."

The voice of the old woman sounded intrigued, for even at first glance the lovely pale face and sari of good material pointed to someone above the coolie class. Moreover, her questing hand had encountered the pendant, which flashed in the last rays of the sun, proclaiming its worth. She hastily thrust it back into the satin folds of Andhra's blouse as Romesh, her son, and Sohan, her nephew, crowded in to see what she had found, for Sohan was a sly youth and not to be trusted.

"How beautiful she is," Romesh murmured in wonder. "What can she be doing all alone in a common ox cart?"

Lalith, his mother, shook her head. "Who can say, my son. But we cannot leave her here at the mercy of snakes or worse. Lift her into the rickshaw and we'll take her to the town. Maybe she will be known there."

So Andhra's still form was placed in the sturdy little vehicle which accompanied them on their travels, pulled by one of the two men. It carried all their possessions—Sohan's basket of snakes for his snake-charming act, Romesh's sitar and drum, a folding tent, food and water and spare clothes. It was also useful in giving old Lalith a lift when she was tired and they were on level or downward-sloping ground.

Both Romesh and Sohan were needed to haul the rickshaw up the stony slope. Lalith glanced keenly about for signs of the driver of the smashed cart. She found him presently, lying near the great boulder, but his neck was broken and he was beyond help, so they left him for the vultures.

The downward track was easy. They reached the river and walked along the rough path until the town was gained. It was now quite dark, and Andhra had still not regained consciousness. There seemed nothing to be done that evening except keep the victim safe.

"She shall sleep in the tent with me," Lalith decided. "By morning she should have regained consciousness and can tell us who she is and where she lives."

So they looked around for a piece of unclaimed ground, and there Romesh set up the minute tent that sheltered his mother each night while he and Sohan slept under the stars, enveloped in a blanket, as did so many of India's poor. It mattered little most of the time, but in the present monsoon period rainstorms were likely to burst upon them without warning, drenching them to the skin.

Lalith kindled a fire with the dry cow dung she had gathered on the way and cooked the evening rice. They ate it squatting on the ground, then settled down for the night, Lalith close to her lovely, silent bedfellow, whom she was already beginning to regard as the daughter she had never borne.

There was no storm tonight. The two men slept in the same comfort as the women and awakened in good temper. Lalith stirred inside the frayed tent and turned curiously to see if the prize flung their way by the gods was now conscious.

The velvety brown eyes were indeed wide open and staring at her in puzzlement. "Where am I?" Andhra asked.

"Do not be afraid, lovely one. We found you lying unconscious on the roadside and brought you with us for your own safety. We are three strolling players who tramp from village to village and manage to make a poor living. Who are you?"

"Andhra." The tone was hesitant and uncertain. Clearly confusion still gripped the mind beneath the shining blue-black hair.

"If you tell us where you live or to where you were traveling, we will help you to reach it," Lalith said.

The smooth brow creased in intense concentration. Andhra tried desperately to recall anything about herself—who she was, to where she had been traveling all alone, from whence she had come; all in vain. A shutter seemed to have descended, leaving her mind a complete blank. She remembered nothing at all of her past life.

Lalith looked concerned. This lovely stranger was undoubtedly suffering from what was known as concussion, brought on by being flung against the unyielding tree trunk. Consciousness had returned and she appeared normal, but memory had gone.

Lalith's skinny fingers moved gently through Andhra's raven locks until they located the expected swelling. As Andhra winced, the old woman nodded. In her travels through remote villages where doctors were unknown, she had picked up a smattering of diagnostic and therapeutic skills that gave some relief to ignorant coolies, and she earned a welcome and a meal for herself and the two young men this way often.

"That hurts?" she said.

Andhra nodded. "My whole head aches and feels as though it were stuffed with cotton wool."

"Do not worry. I can help you, and maybe little by little you will begin to remember the past until everything is clear to you."

Lalith went out to the rickshaw, rummaged among her small bundle of medicines and remedies made from herbs gathered on her wanderings, and came back with a tin of thick green salve. Some of this she plastered on the swelling bruise Andhra had sustained.

"It will help to take away the pain," she explained. "But memory of the past—that is another matter. It may take some time."

She explained the situation to her son and nephew as they ate the breakfast chapatties she had cooked for them. Andhra was persuaded to eat a little, too, but with some reluctance. Obviously this rough and ready sort of existence was far from normal for her. The slender, golden hands were soft, with unblemished almond nails unused to toiling in the fields, drawing water or washing clothes and pots in the river. That, and the jewel around the lovely stranger's neck, convinced Lalith that she came of high caste, which made the mystery of her traveling alone in a decrepit bullock cart even more intriguing.

"We had better leave her with the *burra sahib* and let him find out where she belongs," Sohan said when every crumb had been eaten.

Andhra looked apprehensive. Losing her memory and knowing nothing of her past or future brought acute distress.

Even on so brief an acquaintance, Lalith's was the only face that seemed comforting and kind. She did not want to part from it until the way ahead grew clearer to her.

Her great brown eyes turned beseechingly on the wrinkled, dark face evoked the old woman's pity. "She wishes to stay with me. We could take her with us on our wanderings," she declared.

Sohan laughed disdainfully. "What use would she be? You know each of us must earn his keep. We cannot afford to feed dead weight on the pittance we make."

Lalith stood her ground. The accepted head of the troupe, her views carried weight. Besides, this stranger was no pauper. Had not her questing hands encountered a hidden pouch chinking with rupees while the girl lay unconscious beside her? Then there was also the jewel around her neck. Even more compelling was the need to find a wife for her son as soon as possible. Here, if the gods were kind, was the perfect answer, complete with a dowry.

"She will be no dead weight. Take my word for it," she said firmly.

Romesh, taking his cue from his mother, whose wisdom was proven, looked with dawning favor on Andhra.

"She shall come with us if she wishes. We can see how it works out. Maybe she will remember all in time, and we shall be rewarded by her relatives for befriending her in her time of need."

Sohan, outnumbered, shrugged his thin shoulders and argued no further. The time was coming when he would leave this dominating pair and forge out on his own with his snake-charming act. Then all the rupees he earned would be his alone.

While the two men went off to search for a suitable site to present their show later that day, Andhra helped Lalith with her chores. They washed clothes at the river and spread them on the bank to dry, hoping that no sudden storm would spring up to prevent that. They scoured Lalith's brass cooking pots with sand from the riverbank until they twinkled like gold, filled the water pots and then went off together in search of food.

The open-air market was not far away. Here was a colorful array of vegetables and fruits of all kinds. Lalith filled her coir-string bags with mangoes, bananas, pineapples, beans and red peppers, threading her way through mounds of produce spread out on the ground, the vendors squatting behind them.

Andhra picked her way carefully behind, wrinkling her nose in distaste at the stench rising from the piles of rubbish and rotting vegetables that no one troubled to remove and only the mangy pariah dogs picked over. Noise assailed them from every side. Bullocks bellowed from their long, narrow carts on the edge of the market, demanding food and water; vendors shouted their wares and prices; housewives bargained in shrill voices, beating them down to the last few annas.

It was a relief to pass on to the less noisome spice market. Here, wares were set out in bowls on benches in colorful and aromatic array—powdered nutmeg and black peppercorns, bright red chilis and dried green peppers, fruity chutneys and shredded coconut.

Lalith lingered here, buying a little of this or that from the cheapest source to replenish her spice jars for when they were tramping the countryside, far removed from such refinements.

Andhra, too, enjoyed the intriguing smells and moved on to the grain market with reluctance. Here the wares were in brimming sacks. Brown rice and white, golden maize, dried beans of black, brown, white and every color and size imaginable.

Lalith purchased a quantity of dal, which was a good standby for nourishing meals, a little tea dust and what ghee she could afford, as well as some brown rice and maize flour, which took the last few annas she had.

"It is welcome to have you carry some of the goods back for me," she said, handing one of her bundles to Andhra. "Now we will go, since to wander through the bazaar without rupees only brings longing and unhappiness."

"There is something you want?" Andhra's gaze followed the old woman's, riveted for a moment on the gaudy muslins and silks billowing temptingly from outside the dark little shop on the edge of the cloth-merchants' street.

Lalith shrugged. "It is of no consequence. I can make my sari last for many moons yet."

The sari was faded from the sun and much washing, and close inspection disclosed several mended rents.

"You certainly need material for a new one," Andhra said firmly. "Choose what you will and I will make it for you. I am good at sewing." This much she knew instinctively.

"It must wait. I have no rupees for finery," Lalith demurred.

"I will buy it for you." Just as she knew that she was used to sewing, Andhra knew that she was used to purchasing whatever took her fancy, without question as to whether she could pay for it. Therefore she must have money.

She felt beneath her sari and found the small pouch with its reassuring chink. "Choose what pleases you, and I'll pay. It will be a present for rescuing me when others might have left me to die," she said, leading the way to the Aladdin's cave of gaudy delights.

Lalith's heart swelled with gratitude. Here indeed was a girl with a heart of gold, as well as money with which to indulge her generous impulses. What a splendid wife for her son, if only it could be brought about.

She chose dark blue cotton that would not show the dust and dirt of the roads too quickly, lightened by a few bright flowers. "This I like," she said, smiling.

A length was cut and paid for. Andhra carried it back to the secluded riverside patch where their tent was pitched, and found the two men back before them. Sohan was attending to his snakes while Romesh strummed on his sitar, singing softly to himself in a pleasing baritone.

Lalith and Andhra joined them under the shade of the banyan tree. The former had produced a needle and cotton, so Andhra busied herself with the new material, while the old woman rekindled the cow dung and made tea for them all.

"I have learned a new song," Romesh said presently. "It is very pretty and should please the women and tempt the annas from them. It is really a lullaby, so my voice is too deep for it. Try and pick up the tune, my mother, and then I will teach you the words."

He began to play a simple little tune, monotonous but sweet, humming softly the while. The old woman tried to follow it in a voice that had once been melodious and clear but now creaked a little.

Andhra had stopped sewing. A strange feeling gripped her, a nostalgic waft of faraway, familiar things. Suddenly she was singing in a voice as lovely as herself. The words came instinctively. Somewhere, sometime, she had crooned this lullaby while gently rocking a baby in a cradle.

Romesh's black eyes lit in approval. He played on with added enthusiasm. Lalith and even Sohan paused in their tasks to listen and smile their appreciation. When both instrument and voice had died away, they clapped their hands in pleasure.

"That is good!" Lalith declared. "Your voice is better than mine ever was. We have a new singer in our group, my sons, and now neither of you can say she will not pull her weight in earning her keep."

"No indeed." Romesh's glance lingered on this surprising new acquisition. With all her assets, he would dearly like to have her for his own, yet how could that be? In spite of the strange circumstances in which they had found her, she was clearly far above them in station. Yes, even though she wore not one silver bangle on her golden arms while his mother had three. Neither did she wear a caste mark on her forehead at present, which was even stranger.

"You shall sing for me this evening," he told her. "I have found a good place on the other side of the town. We will walk there as soon as the worst heat has gone."

They tried over several more songs, and Andhra surprised herself with the number of simple tunes and words that came easily to her as soon as Romesh began to play them. Where had she learned them, and for whom? If only they would bring the past flooding back. But there was still a total blackout in her shocked mind.

Then it was time to set off, Sohan carrying his snake basket, Romesh his precious musical instruments.

At first they walked along the riverside, where groups of women pounded clothes on stones while they chattered like magpies, or drew water, which they carried home in pots on their heads with effortless balance. When the main bulk of the town had been passed, they turned away from the river along a narrow street lined with booths with many things for sale. Embroidered slippers vied with garish cottons and brass pots, the owners squatting like ancient gnomes among their wares. Food stalls sent out savory smells, while cobblers fashioned rough sandals from bullock hide for those fortunate enough to be able to spare the rupees, while the majority went barefoot.

At the end of this road was an open space. Coarse grass had sprung up since the start of the rainy season, and a thicket of bamboo made an effective screen at the far end. Here the small band halted. This, being a favorite place for meetings of the townsfolk, would serve equally well for entertainment, Romesh had decided.

He began to bang on his drum to attract the people, while Sohan set down his snake basket and took out his small musical pipe.

Almost immediately children came running, eager for diversion. Soon they were followed by adults, and a considerable crowd had gathered in a ring. Ragged urchins squatted at the front, their elders peering from behind with dark, expectant eyes.

Sohan blew a few soft notes on his pipe, then opened the lid of his basket. As his music swelled to a monotonous rhythmic beat, a large cobra raised its evil head and began to sway in perfect time to the mesmerizing sound.

A gasp of appreciative awe broke from the crowd. They had seen this act many times before, but the magic of the pipe that charmed one of the deadliest of snakes into submission never failed to impress them.

Andhra, too, had witnessed such an exhibition before and knew that there was little danger to expert operators, although a few were caught and fatally injected by the dreaded poison fangs.

Now came the climax of the act. The cobra, excited by its own swaying motion, puffed out its neck until it was dilated into the fearsome hood, with its striking mark that resembled a pair of spectacles. The crowd stared, fascinated, scarcely making a sound lest they divert the attention of the reptile and it should slither from its basket to turn on them.

The pipe music grew softer and began to die away. The dreaded hood deflated. The motion slowed, and finally the snake sank down safely into its basket again.

As Sohan closed the lid, the crowd roared its approval, shouting for more, but it was now the turn of Romesh and Andhra.

His sitar was seductively sweet. The Hindu love song was irresistible. As he glanced at her with an encouraging expression, Andhra began to sing.

Lalith had decked her black hair with golden marigolds and waxy white jasmine, adding the last touch of perfection to her classical beauty. That—and Andhra's attractive voice—caught the imagination of the crowd and held them all spellbound. When the song ended, the people clapped and stamped their pleasure, willing her to sing again. This time she gave them a tender lullaby, chiefly to please the women, and they left her in no doubt of their approval as she finished.

Now the two men sat down with several instruments in front of them—sitar, tabla, flute, drums—and played traditional and classical airs that transported the simple coolies from the drabness of their lives for a brief while, giving them an all-too-rare entertainment that assured a welcome for strolling players wherever they went.

Finally the two men struck up a stirring ballad from Assam, "Sham Bano dooroi," and soon the entire crowd was singing lustily. This brought them to a high pitch of good humor, so that annas came tumbling into the offering bowl before the crowd drifted away to their humble dwellings.

The sun had now set. Darkness would overtake the band before they reached their tent site, but the way was straightforward enough. Sohan marched ahead down to the river, eager to put away his snake and relax. Lalith, Andhra and Romesh followed side by side, more slowly, to suit the pace of the old woman.

Why didn't Romesh walk ahead with Sohan, Andhra reflected, conscious that he pressed too close. The ardent gleam in his eyes when she glanced up at him filled her with unease. Somewhere, in a world far removed from these humble circumstances, she had seen that look in a man's eyes before, but then it had filled her with joy because there had been no barriers between them.

"You did very well this evening," he enthused. "The people like your voice and your lovely face. They have given generously. You will bring prosperity to us, and that is good, because my mother grows older and can no longer please with her singing."

Andhra did not answer. The prospect of endlessly trudging from village to town, literally singing for her supper, brought no joy. Life held more than this. It was all there in the past, if only she could remember.

Night jars began to stir in the casuarina trees fringing the riverbank. Their strange, leafless branches looked like great horse tails in the dusk. Over the water, fireflies swooped and darted, glowing pinpoints in the fading light.

"Hurry!" Sohan called to them. "There is a storm coming."

The heavy humidity of the air certainly suggested it. Before another few yards had been covered, the sky was rent by a jagged flash, thunder roared, and rain came down in torrents.

"My instruments will be ruined," Romesh grumbled, breaking into a run and sprinting ahead, leaving his mother and Andhra to their fate.

It mattered little. The great drops of rain were as warm as a tepid bath, soaking through their flimsy garments and refreshing their perspiring bodies in a most pleasing way. It would have been marvelous to tear them off and run through the rain like the naked stone goddesses on the Hindu temples, she thought, then chided herself for her immodesty.

Where in this great continent, or even the world beyond, had she grown up, to harbor such unmaidenlike thoughts. But then she was no maiden, that much she knew. Somewhere she had loved and been loved in return. Somewhere a life and a man of her own awaited her.

What had happened to leave her stranded, sick in mind and alone in an unfamiliar land? If only she knew.

CHAPTER TEN

How long had she been with the traveling musicians?

Andhra had lost count of time, but the rainy season was drawing to a close. Ahead were the more settled days, when the temperature did not go to such extremes and more rice was planted in the flooded paddy fields, journeys and pilgrimages were undertaken, and life was at its best.

And still she could not remember who she was or what her past circumstances had been.

But it was time to move on, to escape the trap that she felt was closing about her. Lalith was now urging her at every possible moment to marry her son. It was not seemly for Andhra to be traveling with two men in the party unless she were a member of the family or married to one of them, she declared. Normally her son would have been wed before now to someone chosen for him, but as they had always been a traveling group of entertainers, earning a precarious living, this had not proved possible. Now it was high time, and the same applied to Andhra. "I cannot live forever," she pointed out. "I wish to see him settled."

"I may be already married," Andhra objected, to which Lalith shrugged her thin shoulders.

"What self-respecting husband would allow you to roam the countryside alone in a ramshackle bullock cart with an incompetent old driver? And why has no one in the district made a public appeal for a lost wife? Tell me that!"

Andhra was as deeply puzzled herself. She had a vague feeling that she came from somewhere very far off, yet the old woman's words echoed her own fears. Why, if she was someone of any consequence, had no one publicized her disappearance?

Unless, of course, they were searching for her in a totally different state. India was a vast country. East was far removed from west, north from south, the gaps too wide to be bridged easily. They were now in the north center of this sprawling mass, not too far south of Delhi, Lalith told her. There was a vague familiarity about the people, the religion, the Urdu language spoken locally, that suggested she had once lived here— but where, and how long ago? It was frightening to be so ignorant of all that lay in her past.

About half the rupees originally in her hidden purse were still there. Now was the time to break away, before she was quite destitute and reduced to begging, she decided. If she could reach the capital, there was a chance that she might get work there, perhaps as a teacher of children. She could read all the notices in public places and any newspaper that fell into her hands, an accomplishment that filled Lalith with admiration and set her apart from coolies and the common people.

The decisive moment came one morning when they were camped on the outskirts of an impressive city near a railway track. Steam trains puffed noisily by from time to time, filling the air with acrid smoke and falling soot. Lalith and the two men did not seem to mind, but Andhra found this traveling life, living from hand to mouth in precarious, often uncomfortable circumstances, less and less to her taste. True, the rainy season, when she was too often soaked to the skin, was passing, but there was still the indignity of having to stand up and sing for the crowd most evenings, whether she felt like it or not. Now, in addition, Lalith expected her to dance.

"The crowd likes that best of all, and it charms the coins from them better than anything," the old woman said. From a rush basket in the rickshaw she unearthed a vivid red sari spangled with gold and silver. "I have not used it these past few years. My joints are too stiff to bend and sway. But you, my pretty one, will look a real *begum* in it. Come, I will teach you."

Attired in the showy garment, Andhra was coerced into posturing and posing, stamping her feet and gesticulating with her expressive hands, while Romesh played seductively and Sohan eyed her with undisguised lust in his black eyes. The experience disturbed her deeply. She felt degraded being made to prance and posture, showing off her desirable figure for the titillation of men. Somewhere, long ago, perhaps in another incarnation, she had been the spectator at just such displays, watching men drool over the performers and feeling herself far above such antics. Now she was forced into it herself.

And Lalith was quite right about the inadvisability of traveling in such primitive circumstances with two unmarried men in the party. Romesh was becoming quite bold in the way he treated her, while the undisguised lust in Sohan's expression filled her with apprehension.

"We should do well here today, with the festival beginning," Lalith said as they ate their chapatties. "With a holiday from work, the crowds will be in a generous mood and ready to give. They will be glad of entertainment while waiting for the big performance this evening, so you must sing and dance your best, my pretty one, and then we shall have chicken curry tonight, and sweetmeats to follow."

It sounded a veritable feast after their usual monotonous diet, but it brought little response from Andhra. Her mind was firmly on escape, and the best time to get away from a situation that was fast becoming a trap to ensnare her for life. With Lalith her constant shadow, it would be difficult but not impossible.

This was the day, and this evening the hour. There might not be so good a chance again. This city of Ranchi was noted for its festival, Romesh declared. The maharaja himself attended on his state elephant to open the proceedings and watch the performance of the Ramayanah, which finished with a display of fireworks. Crowds would flock in the thousands for such excitement, and it would be easy to slip away from Lalith and be lost in the throng. She would make her way to the railway station and there wait for a train to Delhi. Once in the capital, surely work could be found more congenial than this endless wandering and the threat of being tied for life to a man she did not love.

With high hopes of a substantial collection, the small band of entertainers made their way in the early afternoon to where the stage had been set up for the evening performance. Already the throng was dense. They milled around the stage like swarming ants or squatted patiently farther back, waiting for the free show to begin on this, the highlight of the year.

"Some of them will be glad of entertainment until the big performance begins," Lalith declared, taking up a stand in the first small space she could find. "Let your drum speak, my son, to draw their attention."

They set down their props, and Romesh began to pound as loudly as he could, while Sohan proclaimed the delights of their offerings in a penetrating voice.

"You look a true *begum* and will please them well," Lalith murmured to Andhra, glancing with satisfaction at the shimmering red sari spangled with gold and silver, the lovely golden face, the shining crown of hair decked with fragrant flowers. "Do not be shy but dance as though you were performing for the maharaja himself."

Pray heaven it would be for the last time, Andhra reflected, squirming inwardly because she felt that displaying her charms for the men was even more degrading than singing for her supper.

She did both very well, to the gratification of the crowd that drifted around, backed up by Sohan's snake act and music and songs from the men and herself. At the conclusion a shower of annas descended into their offering bowl, so that Lalith clasped her bony hands together in satisfaction and babbled of the feast they would have the following day.

Then came a great shout from some of the people, taken up by all the vast throng until the noise was deafening. The maharaja was arriving on his state elephant to open the proceedings and watch the performance.

The crowd surged forward, carrying Lalith and her group with it. For a moment Andhra had a good view of the awesome spectacle, and she gasped at the magnificence of it. The elephant, walking sedately under the guidance of its mahout, perched on the beast's neck, was scarcely visible under its magnificent trappings and bunting. High on its back it carried the howdah, all cream and gold, surmounted by a great golden umbrella fringed with cream tassels. In the place of honor sat the maharaja, hands raised, palms together before his face in the position of greeting, nodding and smiling to his people from right to left. His golden turban flashed with precious stones, while his satin robes shimmered like a rainbow in the light of flares carried in the vanguard. Behind him squatted his bodyguard, a stately figure carrying his staff of honor.

Just one breathtaking glimpse, then the crowd surged back to make way for the procession, carrying Andhra and Lalith with it.

Sudden, startling emotion gripped Andhra's mind. Somewhere, in some former incarnation perhaps, she herself had ridden thus, graciously bowing, applauded by the crowd, queen of all she surveyed. If only she could remember where and when.

The elephant made its stately way to the small stage and circled three times slowly around it. Then the maharaja paid his respects to the gods represented by the actors and so ensured good fortune for the coming year for all the townsfolk.

Then the ruler was assisted down and took the chair of honor in front of the stage, surrounded by his retinue. Now the play could begin.

The story of Rama as it unfolded was vaguely familiar to Andhra. Somewhere she had seen it before. The actors, all boys under the age of fourteen, sumptuously dressed in brocades and satins and lavishly sprinkled with jewels, played their parts with gusto, enacting the Ramayana through all its twists and turns, to the exciting climax where the lost Sita is found and she and Rama are reunited, to the thunderous applause of the crowd.

Acute nostalgia gripped Andhra. Could she, too, be a lost princess? But where was her prince, and the happy ending?

Glancing at Lalith applauding as vigorously as any, she came down to earth with a bump. Far from being a princess, she was reduced to being a humble strolling player in danger of being forced into a marriage she did not want. Now if ever, with this surging crowd about them, was the time to slip away and escape to the railway station and freedom.

Of Romesh and Sohan there was no sign. They had become separated and lost to view in the sea of humanity. Lalith's attention was all on the effigy of the demon king, a giant figure constructed of bamboo and colored paper at the rear of the stage. Stuffed with fireworks, it was now due to be lit, to disintegrate in a shower of sparks and smoke, symbolically destroying the power of evil. In the turmoil of this added diversion, she could escape without detection.

With a bang and a roar the monstrous figure erupted like an exploding volcano. The crowd stamped and shrieked its approval as an avalanche of stars rose and fell in a cascade behind the stage. Lalith had eyes for nothing but the spectacle. Silently Andhra thrust herself into the crowd, trying to push her way back out to freedom.

But the whole throng was intent on pushing the other way, forward, to extract the last bit of drama from the fireworks and see the departure of the maharaja on his splendid mount. Andhra was swept with it as the mass surged forward.

Twisting and turning, she managed to propel herself to the front of the crowd, far enough from where she had left Lalith to be quite lost to view.

"Make way for his eminence the maharaja!" called the guards, striding forward and pushing back the crowd with their long bamboo poles, to form a wide pathway for the royal entourage.

Confused by the flaring torches and harassed both by the guards and the shifting crowd, Andhra desperately continued to force her way on, putting as much distance as possible between herself and Lalith before the mass of people disintegrated and drifted away, depriving her of coverage. Blind to everything except the need to escape, she took risks foreign to her usual common sense.

A mishap was inevitable. She had almost thrust her way through the crowd to freedom when an overbold dart forward brought her into contact with a guard's pole, flailing from side to side. It caught her sharply on the ankle, bringing searing pain and sick giddiness. With a gasp of agony she slumped down in the path of the guards and the advancing state elephants.

With angry shouts the guards halted the procession. Through a daze of pain, Andhra heard the commanding voice of the maharaja. "What is the trouble?"

"This woman, your eminence," one of them explained. "She ignored my warning to keep back and darted out. She was struck by my cane. It was her own fault."

The guards stood aside as the royal mahout urged his elephant forward so that his master could see for himself what was happening.

"Is she hurt?" The ruler peered down from his lofty perch, vexed at this unfortunate ending to a joyful festival, no doubt.

One of the guards kneeled beside Andhra, probing her ankle. She winced at his touch and sharply drew in her breath.

"Her ankle may be broken, your eminence. It is doubtful if she can stand or walk."

"Where are her family? Is there no one to take charge of her?"

At this Andhra was sharply reminded of the group from which she was trying to escape. To be handed back to them was unthinkable. With an effort she sat up, turning a beseeching face toward the splendid figure above.

"I have no family, sir, nor any home. Please have me taken to some place of refuge where I may rest and recover. I have rupees. I can pay."

As the light of a flare fell squarely on her, fully illuminating her lovely face and lustrous hair garlanded with flowers, the maharaja uttered an exclamation of astonishment. He stared transfixed, as though he had seen a ghost, and finally he uttered a gruff command.

"Hoist her to the rear elephant. She shall have shelter in the palace until her difficulties are over."

As she was lifted and placed in the howdah, which was occupied by two of the ruler's state officials, Andhra breathed a sigh of relief. She was safe now from having to degrade herself by singing and dancing for the masses; safe from a forced marriage, the thought of which filled her with revulsion. Lalith and the two men were too far behind to have witnessed the scene. They would only realize her defection when the crowd had all melted away.

The royal procession now continued on its stately way, leaving first the crowd and then the town behind and finally reaching the palace on the hill. An imposing structure of domes and arches topped by soaring cupolas, it stood in aloof isolation on neglected grounds.

The maharaja, elderly and stiff beneath his fine robes, climbed down with the aid of elephant steps and disappeared within the great portal. He had evidently given instructions regarding Andhra, for she was lifted down and carried by two of the guards through echoing passages and rooms to an apartment at the rear of the palace, clearly in the women's quarters.

Yet this part had an unused, deserted air, quite devoid of the shrill voices and childish bickering characteristic of these places. Had the maharaja been a younger, more virile man, Andhra would have concluded that she had been brought here for his gratification, perhaps to be kept as a concubine for her alluring face and figure. But he was clearly quite elderly, his august face lined with sorrow and adversity, in spite of his high rank. Moreover, there was the strange astonishment that had flashed over his face as he peered closely down at her, as though he had seen her before.

What could it mean? Was this aging ruler and this splendid crumbling palace part of the blank past that so tantalizingly eluded her?

As she lay pondering on the faded brocade couch, an old woman glided in. "I am Mira, an old ayah, the only woman left in the palace," she mumbled through toothless gums. "I have been sent to help you."

She bent over the couch, peering with her failing eyes into the sweet young face below. Then she, too, exhibited the same reaction as her master, but to a greater degree.

"The maharani has returned, her beauty undimmed after all these years," she muttered fearfully in a tongue that Andhra could just follow. "This is a miracle."

Then her eyes caught the gleam of gold and jewels as, disarranged by the transportation, the star escaped the folds of the sari and hung exposed on its gold chain. The old woman fell stiffly to her knees, clasping her hands together in front of her face.

"*Namaste,* my mistress. There is no doubt of your identity, for you wear the Star of Randevi, the emblem of this noble house. I must hasten to inform his eminence at once." Rising with an effort, she hobbled from the room, leaving Andhra in a state of mounting tension.

Surely she could not be anything so exalted as a maharani, the wife of this sorrowful old man. Surely her own vague dreams of a virile young prince and a laughing baby could not be entirely a mirage.

Was she going mad or was the whole world insane, she wondered desperately. If the truth was not revealed soon, she certainly would go out of her mind with sheer frustration.

CHAPTER ELEVEN

In stunned silence Andhra lay on the faded couch, the pain of her ankle almost forgotten. Could she really be connected with this crumbling palace and its august ruler? That could explain her beauty, her refinement, her good-quality sari and the shame she had felt in being forced to dance and sing for the masses, but not other aspects of the puzzle. If she belonged here, why had not her disappearance been published, and why had she been traveling in a decrepit bullock cart when her first accident occurred, instead of in a style more befitting her rank.

Above all, where was that shadowy, thrilling male figure who haunted her dreams, filling her with tormented longing. Surely he could not be just a faceless phantom borne of her imagination.

She was not kept long in doubt before the door was thrust open to admit the maharaja, old Mira hobbling in his wake. He strode straight to the couch, bent and took the jeweled star in his plump white hand, studying it intensely.

"The Star of Randevi," he murmured incredulously at last. "The gods have relented and given me back my lost daughter."

"You can't mean that I was born here, in this place," Andhra faltered. "How could I be lost for months, wandering around with strolling players, without being recognized and claimed?"

"Strolling players!" The maharaja looked shocked. "What brought you to such straits, my daughter?"

Andhra shook her head in puzzlement. "I was involved in an accident that resulted in concussion and robbed me of all memory of things that happened before. A band of strolling players found me and took pity on me. I became one of them, but I loathed singing and dancing for the crowds and was trying to escape from them when I was struck by your guard's cane."

The great man sank down on a chair beside the couch as though his limbs were weak with astonishment. "I am as much in the dark regarding your past life as you, my child."

"I don't understand."

"How could you? You were given away as a small child. Tell me, are you still named Andhra?"

She nodded.

"Then that is all I know of you. All these years I have been robbed of your beauty, youth and companionship through my own folly, picturing you living far away in England, not daring to make too many inquiries because I was ashamed of my past. I felt the gods were punishing me for trying to outwit them."

"Why did Mira mistake me for the maharani?"

"Because, my daughter, you are so amazingly like your mother was as my young wife. Mira in her superstitious ignorance thought you had been reincarnated, as youthful and lovely as ever, but that, of course, is impossible. She died many years ago, leaving me desolate."

"I think you owe it to me to tell me the whole story," Andhra said, wincing as a slight movement brought pain shooting through her ankle. "At least as far as your part goes."

"I shall indeed be glad to pour it all out, now that the gods have worked this miracle. It will ease my desolate heart and bring me comfort. But first your injured ankle must be attended to, my child. I will send Vishvonathan, my faithful attendant, to you. He is wise and skilled in the healing arts and will make you more comfortable. Then I will command that you be brought to my suite of rooms, where you will dine with me, and I shall open my heart to you."

The bearded Vishvonathan soon appeared. With gentle touch he probed Andhra's injury, pronounced a hairline crack, bound it firmly and told her that it must be rested for the next week while it healed itself.

After he had gone, Mira bathed Andhra's face and hands in warm, scented water, combed her lustrous hair and twisted it into a becoming knot at the nape of her neck, then surrendered her to the two servants who entered with a litter.

Swiftly she was carried through corridors to be set down on a cushioned divan in the maharaja's private suite. She found herself in sumptuous splendor, the walls covered with silken panels depicting scenes from the Ramayana along with sylvan settings of lakes and mountains and beautiful gardens. Deep-pile carpets masked the mosaic floor, while lustrous hangings and cushions everywhere lent an air of soft comfort.

The house bearers placed a round table beside the divan on which they set out a meal of rich and varied small dishes, then silently left the room. The maharaja sat on the padded low stool on the opposite side of the table and looked at his new-found daughter with profound wonder.

"It seems like a dream," he said at last. "I am unworthy of such bounty of the gods, but you, my lost one, deserve all I can give you to make up for my past mistakes."

They each helped themselves from the many dishes, a veritable feast to Andhra, who had grown used to the restricted fare of the masses. When they had finished, the dishes were cleared and fragrant tea was brought in a silver pot. It was then that the maharaja of Randevi began to fill in at least some of her shadowy past.

"A quarter of a century seems to have rolled away," he murmured with a sigh. "For it was thus that my dear wife and I used to sit of an evening. How happy we were, especially when we knew she was to bear my child. Like all high-born Indians, I longed for a son above everything, to take my place when I had gone to the abode of the gods."

Andhra nodded. A son. She, too, knew the triumphant pride that a son of one's own can bring. Surely it could not be merely a dream.

"Perhaps I should be blessed twice over, I thought," her father went on, "for like all my peers, I had several concubines hidden away in the women's quarters. The youngest was my favorite, and she, too, was to bear a child around the same time."

It was the custom, Andhra reflected. Wives accepted it as such with as good a grace as possible.

"Strangely enough, both my women went into labor on the same day, and that night two new beings were born of my loins. The concubine produced a perfect male child, but to my mortification, my wife bore a daughter—you."

Andhra sighed in sympathy, for when it came to inheritance, legitimate offspring usually took precedence over others, yet daughters could not carry on the direct line.

"Your chief consolation must have been the hope of your wife bearing a son later on," she said.

He shook his head, gray beneath its snowy turban. "Even that hope was denied me, for by some malignant trick of evil spirits, both women had a difficult birth. The young concubine lost too much blood and died the following day. Your mother survived, but only just, and the physician said she would bear no more children."

"You must have felt devastated."

"Near demented, I fear," he said ruefully, "for on the spur of the moment I acted foolishly and unjustly. The perfect little boy child was smuggled into the lavish bed of my wife, while you—my puny, plain little daughter—were whisked to the concubines' quarters."

"Plain and puny!" Andhra grimaced in disbelief.

"You were then, strange as it seems now, with your grace and beauty to challenge the goddesses. The few people who knew the truth were sworn to secrecy on pain of death. Even your mother never knew the truth but thought she had borne me the son I desired."

"But when and why did you give me away, my father? No doubt I should have grown up quite happily in the women's quarters."

"No doubt, my child, but as you grew and began to toddle around, you changed completely and became so like a tiny edition of your beautiful mother that the truth could no longer be concealed. I realized that you must be banished from the concubines' quarters, where your mother occasionally went, before you grew any older and she and everyone else realized the truth. For by now she idolized the boy, Amjad, whom she believed to be her own baby. It would have caused a rift between us had she learned of my deception."

"So what did you do with me?" Andhra's voice sounded wistful and strained.

"Why, nothing to harm you, my child. There was a garrison of the East India Company regiment stationed here at the time, and I was on friendly terms with one of the officers. We used to have some great games of chess here in the palace. Then he learned that he was to be transferred to Chandipur, which is a long way off from here, so we should see little of each other."

The maharaja paused as though thinking back, then went on. "He came to dinner on his last evening, and during the conversation between us, he mentioned that he had no son, only a baby daughter."

"She'll grow up a lonely only child," he said and sighed. "For my wife seems so debilitated by this hot climate that it's too risky to try to have any more.

"It was then that the idea came to me," Andhra's father continued. "I knew that the British had a more liberal outlook on life where wives and daughters were concerned. I felt that you would be happier growing up in a loving small family with a step-father and step-mother than shut away with concubines who might be jealous of your beauty as you grew older and mistreat you. I asked him if he and his wife would care to adopt a sister for their only child, and told him the whole story in confidence."

Chandipur. The name seemed to ring a bell in Andhra's mind, but it was vague and she could not grasp the significance.

"I had you brought in to show to him," her father was continuing, "sleepy and enchanting from your cot. He was delighted with you and said his wife would love you as much as their own baby, and that you could be brought up together and educated in England. It seemed the best thing for you and for all of us, so he took you home wrapped in a shawl, assuring me that he would never divulge the secret of your birth. The following day he and his regiment were transferred to Chandipur, and I never saw either of you again. Chandipur was badly hit in the mutiny about twenty years later, and I felt sure neither of you could have survived the terrible siege of the fort, which was practically wiped out."

Again Andhra grasped at the name Chandipur, and again its significance eluded her. Absently she fingered the Star of Randevi on its golden chain.

"It is a miracle that you still have it," her father said. "It was placed around your neck at birth, indicating that you were of this royal house, but I asked Major Hilton to keep it in a safe place for you, at least until you grew up."

Major Hilton. Another ringing of a bell, all to no purpose. If only she could remember clearly all that had happened in those twenty lost years.

"What can I do to help you recall everything?" her father said in concern. "Have you no recollection of a garrison town and living in a dak bungalow with a British regimental family and Indian servants?"

Andhra thought hard. "There seems to be a vague figure of Ayah who cared for me," she said slowly, "but only for a brief spell. I think I must have been sent to school in England, a strange, cold land where customs are different. I seem to understand them as clearly as our own customs."

The maharaja nodded encouragingly. "That would almost certainly have been the case, under the circumstances. And afterward, my child, when the native troops rebelled against their British overlords and the mutiny, one of the most terrible episodes in Indian history, broke out, the usurpers, as they were then termed, were slaughtered in hundreds and the land ran red with blood."

As he spoke, Andhra began to feel her own blood run cold. Nameless horrors and terrible fears possessed her. Undoubtedly she had been caught up in the mutiny and deeply scarred by its consuming fire. Yet one being seemed to stand out head and shoulders above the welter of horror—a godlike being whose shadowy presence filled her heart with burning desire and utter longing.

"My prince," she murmured wonderingly at last. "My brave, noble prince. He was there once, but where is he now?"

"Can you recall his name, my child?"

She shook her head, and now the tears started in her dark

eyes, for he had meant the world to her, and she could not bear to lose him forever.

Her father pressed her hand in sympathy. "Do not despair. Already you vaguely recall a little of those lost years. One day I am sure the dark curtain in your mind will be torn aside and everything will be clear again. It only needs the right key to unlock the mystery. If only you could recall the name of the prince entangled in your past, that might help. To be sure, India is a vast country and has spawned many princes. Some of them lost their power after the mutiny and faded into obscurity, but perhaps if investigations were made in the Chandipur area, something might come to light."

She nodded. "What became of my mother and the boy she believed to be her own son?" she asked, going off on a tangent. "You seem to be the only person of consequence in the palace. Even the women's quarters are deserted."

He grimaced. "What would I want of concubines at my age? Since the gods dealt me such a blow, I have become almost a recluse. The festival is the only occasion on which I fulfill my princely role, and that is chiefly so as not to disappoint my people. Your mother and the boy she believed to be her own son are both dead," he ended sadly.

"Tell me about it." Since she had never known them, she could feel no sense of loss, but it certainly affected her own position.

"My son, as was the custom with his contemporaries, was keen on big-game shooting. He was brave and reckless and took too many risks. He was killed by a tiger three years ago."

"And my mother?"

"Shock and grief brought her low. She could neither eat nor sleep and went off in a decline soon after."

"I'm sorry. Your life has been hard in spite of your wealth and rank." She sighed.

He nodded. "But now I have found you, it will be better. You are all I have in the world, my long-lost daughter. I am no longer so wealthy as formerly, since the British annexed some of my possessions, but I am wealthy enough to give you a life of luxury here with me."

A feeling of vague dissatisfaction gripped her. This was not really what she wanted. Somewhere, sometime, she had led a fulfilling life of her own. She was convinced it was there waiting for her, if only she could find it again.

"You are kind, my father, and I'm grateful to you. When I was with the troupe, longing to escape but not knowing where to go, this timely refuge would have seemed a heaven-sent haven. It still does, but that doesn't mean I can settle here with you and dismiss the past from my mind. Somewhere out in the world I led a full life of my own, I feel sure. Maybe there was even a husband and children. And that makes it all the more strange that I should be wandering abroad in a dilapidated ox cart and that no one has made any inquiry or a search for me. I'm sure you'll understand that I can never rest until I've solved the baffling mystery of my blank past."

He nodded slowly. "I do understand, my child. I shall do all I can to help, for believe me, I am just as concerned as you to know all that was happening to you while I thought you had been killed in the mutiny. Now tell me everything you can clearly remember regarding how you came to be with that troupe."

"Nothing," she said with a sigh. "They found me lying by the roadside unconscious, a wrecked ox cart nearby. I'd been flung against a tree, and that caused my concussion and loss of memory. It was many miles east of here. We wandered all through the rainy season, sleeping anywhere we could find shelter."

Her father shook his head in perplexity. "I cannot bear to think of it. Maybe the gods will help if I pray hard enough, or perhaps my wise attendant, Vishvonathan, who is skilled in the arts of healing, will know how to bring your memory back."

Vishvonathan was immediately sent for, and entered with a deferential bow to his master and the beautiful princess, who, like a character from the Ramayana, had dramatically returned from the dead to gladden her father's desolate heart.

When he had heard what little there was to tell, he said decisively, "Since the loss of memory was brought on by the shock of collision with a tree, only another shock is likely to bring it back, my master."

"A physical shock, you mean?"

"Not necessarily. A mental shock could possibly bring the

past flooding back, providing it was profound enough, and part of this blank past."

The maharaja sighed. "Where do we begin to make inquiries in this vast country of ours?"

Vishvonathan sank his head deep into his hands and remained silent awhile, thinking deeply. At last he raised it, a faraway look in his eyes. "The princess does not belong to any state in this part of India, my master. I see in my mind's eye an aura of the faroff south surrounding her."

"Then we must concentrate our efforts there." The maharaja frowned as though trying to grasp something elusive. "I seem to recall some prince appealing for information regarding his missing wife," he said at last. "It was in the *Indian Express* newspaper, Delhi edition. The prince lived in the south, I believe, but it was some moons ago and I took little notice of it."

Andhra clasped her hands in supplication. "Oh, Father, if only you can follow it up, perhaps it will turn out to be the clue we are looking for!"

He glanced at her flushed face and feverishly bright eyes. "It shall be done, my child, by Vishvonathan and myself. In the meantime, you are to rest in peace, to restore your injured ankle and the vitality you lost in your unaccustomed rough living. Mira shall prepare a fitting bedchamber for you and wait on you hand and foot. You are to forget everything and leave it to us, in case this clue leads nowhere. If we have any success, you will know soon enough."

With this Andhra had to be content. After her recent hard life, it was heaven to presently lie between silken sheets in a soft bed, with no irksome dancing and singing to oppress her and every want promptly attended to by the adoring Mira. This was the life to which she was accustomed, she knew without question. Once her expressive hands had been soft, with tinted almond nails and not a blemish to mar them—the kind of hands to fondle a baby or caress a passionate lover in a way that made his smoldering desire burst into consuming flame.

These things she had known with joy in that elusive past and would know again, however long it took to find them. As for her hands, Mira, anointing them with salve made from almond oil, had promised they would soon lose the blemishes acquired by carrying water and washing clothes at the river's edge.

"Under my care you will become again as beautiful and alluring as Sita, the goddess princess," she boasted. "Tomorrow you will wear a sari fit to match the Star of Randevi, and then no man will look on you without desire."

Smiling at the thoughts conjured up, Andhra fell asleep in her newfound luxury.

CHAPTER TWELVE

Ranjana squared his splendid shoulders, flicked the reins and urged his horse on faster up the slope that seemed to wind on and on without end.

He had forgotten how exacting the road to Darjeeling was, and how atrocious. What a wonderful service the railway would give when it was finally completed. Small wonder that Jenny was so proud of her husband, Mark Copeland, and the marvelous feat of engineering of which he was in charge. Courageous, farsighted and immensely practical, Mark was one of the finest Englishmen to be found, and Ranjana greatly looked forward to seeing him again.

Yet if Mark and Jenny were pioneers, he himself and Andhra were equally dedicated, Ranjana reflected. The tea plantations taking shape in the neglected south would, when they came to fruition, bring equal benefits to a vast region that had for too long been left to rot in the humid heat, ruled by avaricious and corrupt men like his uncle, Balbir Mukti, nawab of Cochpur. It suited such men very well to let the coolies and their families muddle on as they had done for centuries in their wretched hovels, wresting a precarious living from their pitiful plots and scrawny livestock, wringing taxes from the few rupees they managed to make, while giving nothing themselves.

But if he himself succeeded in establishing a flourishing new industry on his estate and proved that tea could be grown on the southern *ghats* as well as in Darjeeling or Ceylon, it would encourage others to start up. Foreign capital would pour in, and enterprising companies that would operate more justly and pay fair wages. The coolies would no longer be forced to live from hand to mouth, starving in flood time and dying in droughts. The tea plantations on the hill slopes would be prop-

erly irrigated to ensure water at all times, and eventually the
necessary pumping gear could be installed.

It would all take time. Would his own limited capital stretch
to all that would be required for this development, and keep
wages going until the tea bushes could start yielding a worthwhile return? It must. He was determined to make the project
succeed, and Andhra had been equally keen.

Brave, beautiful Andhra. His heart sank as he thought of her
and the reason for this journey that had forced him away from
the estate when he could ill be spared. Only the threat of
danger to his beloved could have pried him away at this critical
time, leaving Robert to carry the responsibility alone.

She had set off for Darjeeling cheerfully enough, happy at
the thought of being reunited with little Sanjay and bringing
him and Ayah back to the Summer Palace. At first, though he
was greatly missing her, he had immersed himself in estate
business, consoling himself that he would soon have both his
wife and son back with him. When time passed and they did
not come, he sent a telegram to far Darjeeling asking why.

The result had been a profound shock. Jenny had answered
that she was mystified by his message. She had neither seen nor
heard anything of Andhra and had not even known her sister
was on the way to collect her son.

Immediately Ranjana had handed over the reins to Robert
and set off for Darjeeling, determined to move heaven and
earth to resolve the mystery. Terrible fears beset him. The
train seemed to crawl when he wished it to fly. He could
neither eat nor sleep and irked his fellow first-class passengers
with his restlessness.

After Calcutta progress had been even more frustrating,
until now at last he was on the final stretch, urging his weary
horse beyond its capabilities.

Why had he allowed Andhra to travel alone, he reflected for
the umpteenth time. She was worth more than any plantation.
He should have let things slide and gone with her. He recalled
how she had set off, soberly dressed and without jewelry so as
not to attract unwelcome attention. Yet nothing could hide the
grace and beauty of the golden face half veiled by the gauzy
scarf about it.

Here at last was Darjeeling. He heaved a deep sigh of relief as the red roofs of the so-British bungalows came into sight. They made a picture to stir the senses, set among pleasant gardens and shrubberies and flanked by the deep green of tea terraces. Even more breathtaking was the backdrop of the Himalayas, rising sharply majestic and capped by glistening snow.

But Ranjana was in no mood to appreciate beauty. He pressed on to the bungalow where Mark and Jenny lived, thankfully dismounted and handed the reins to an Indian servant.

Jenny had heard him arrive. She flung open the door without waiting for the houseboy. There she stood to greet him, with Ayah pressing close behind, little Sanjay crowing in her arms. "Andhra? She is not here? You have heard nothing?" Ranjana said tersely, taking both her hands and gripping them too firmly in his anxiety.

He knew by her expression that she had no good news for him. Her small face looked pinched, her eyes haunted.

She shook her head. "Every day since your message came to say you were on your way, I have hoped that she would turn up or at least send some word, but all to no purpose. Each day my anxiety deepens. Something quite drastic must have happened to her between Madras and here. What, I dread to think."

"I too." His handsome face was haggard with fatigue and despair. He looked crushed by a blow against which even his indomitable will had no power. Even the sight of his chubby little son could do nothing to lighten the load.

Deeply sorry for him, Jenny rallied her own forces, drew him inside and crisply asked Ayah to order tea and refreshments immediately.

"You look as though you've scarcely slept or eaten since setting off," she said. "We can't afford to have you crack up just now. We must think of some positive measure to try and trace her, instead of waiting passively any longer."

He somberly agreed but allowed himself to be pressed into an easy chair in the comfortable, very English-looking sitting room. Jenny was quite right. He needed all his resources to fight this nightmare and bring it to a successful end, if it was humanly possible.

The superb Darjeeling tea was infinitely refreshing, and at her insistence he mechanically ate the little rice cakes she thrust upon him.

"Now you must rest for an hour or two until dinner," she declared. "Mark will be home by then, and we can discuss what to do over the meal."

Too crushed to argue and dropping with fatigue, he made no objection but followed her to the simple guest room he and Andhra had occupied for a short time after their marriage. Looking at the bed that dominated the room with its English feather mattress into which a tired body sank luxuriously in this cool Himalayan climate, he clenched his lips in impotent longing. He would gladly have given all he possessed to see her lying there, waiting for him in all her beauty.

He flung off his clothes, glancing through the window before turning to the bed. How attractive the large garden was, the flowers and shrubs growing riotously and healthily in this cool, moist climate. So different from the Summer Palace, where without the constant attention of a gardener, it would have been impossible to keep plants alive between the rainy seasons.

Conditions were better on the hill slopes, where the tea plantations were taking shape, but even there he was pressing on with an irrigation scheme. Depressingly, everything took so long in this land of rigid bureaucracy and weather-induced lethargy. For one schooled in Western ways, it was bitterly frustrating, especially with plans constantly bedeviled by that vile Balbir in addition.

In spite of the load on his mind, exhaustion brought sleep and a respite, until some time later he was roused by Jenny peeping in at the door. "It seems a great shame to wake you, but dinner is ready and Mark has been home for half an hour," she murmured. "And I've recalled something that might possibly hold a clue to Andhra's whereabouts. I'll tell you when you come down."

"You have!" With a great surge of hope, Ranjana leaped up, careless of his nakedness, as Jenny closed the door and fled.

He doused himself with cold water in the bathroom alcove. Whereas in the south it was always tepid, here it was icy and brought a gasp. But a vigorous toweling left him glowing all over, and in spite of the care gnawing at him, he felt a great deal better for both it and the brief sleep.

He greeted Mark warmly, asked how the railroad was progressing, and received the inevitable answer in this country.

"Slower than I'd like, but we'll finish someday, by hook or by crook."

"If he doesn't finish himself first," Jenny declared half seriously. "He works such long hours, I'm a real grass widow."

For a moment Ranjana caught a glimpse of her secret soul, full of a yearning she scarcely understood. Small and delicate, she had always craved companionship and someone to lean on. In the old days it had been Andhra. Surely Mark could see and make allowances, delegate his great project a little more to underlings and lavish a little more time on her.

Or give her a baby to love and cherish. Whose fault was it that as yet they were childless? Surely not Mark's, as tough and rugged as his job. Poor Jenny must be that most pitiful of mortals, a barren woman.

Ranjana thought with pride of his own lusty son and nubile consort, then sobered again at the reality of events. "What were you going to tell me that might possibly give a clue to this intolerable mystery?" he asked when they were seated and being served with lentil soup.

"Oh yes, but don't expect too much to come of it. It is just an idea that may lead nowhere, but we can't ignore anything at all that might give us an idea of where Andhra may be."

"Emphatically not."

"It goes right back to the old days before the mutiny," Jenny said reflectively. "We had a dear old ayah before we went off to school in England. She loved us both, but Andhra she almost worshipped, perhaps because she was of the same race."

Ranjana kept his impatience in check, listening intently.

"Ayah was still with the household when we returned years later, but she left hurriedly soon after to care for a sick daughter. That was around the time the mutiny broke out," Jenny continued. "After that, of course, everything was chaos and horror. We heard no more of Ayah and never expected to."

"Yet you did, quite recently. Andhra mentioned a letter you had received here. I'd forgotten all about it in the press of events, until now," he said, thinking back. "I remember Andhra saying she must answer it and send a present, but I doubt if she managed it, what with one thing and another."

"Exactly. The thought has just crossed my mind—could she have decided to break her journey at Calcutta and go in person for a last glimpse of Ayah? The letter said the old woman could not live much longer."

Ranjana nodded. "That would be typical of warmhearted Andhra, and if she made up her mind on the spur of the moment, that would account for her not saying anything to me before she left. As for you, you didn't even know she was on her way here, did you, so she would have had no qualms about your being worried by her nonarrival."

"That's right. It would have been quite feasible for her to make a snap decision. And on reaching the convent, possibly Ayah prevailed on her to stay for a while on the plea that it would not be for long."

"Possibly." He sounded doubtful. Andhra would scarcely have lingered so long at the convent without getting in touch with Jenny or him. However, any lead was better than none and must be followed to a decisive end.

"I shall start for the convent first thing tomorrow," he declared on a slightly more optimistic note. "If you give me the address, I'll find the place. Not so far off from Chandipur, your old garrison home, I believe. Don't forget I grew up in that district. The memories are painful as well as pleasant. My family were dubbed traitors in the mutiny for consorting with the British. Our palace was looted and half destroyed. My elder brother partly restored it and lives there now in a subdued style. I must pay him a flying visit while I have the chance, or he will be deeply offended."

Jenny was greatly relieved to hear the note of optimism in his voice and see him looking more purposeful. Even if this chance came to nothing, action was so much better for him than passive waiting.

"I shall also advertise in a discreet way in several newspapers, and inform the authorities, if nothing comes of this clue," he went on. "But let us hope it need never come to that. I pray to all the gods of my fathers that I may find her at the convent."

"Let it be so!" Jenny augmented. "Now try one of these grilled trout. They are from a cool mountain lake, and my cook does them to perfection. You have nothing so good in the south."

Even under stress he enjoyed the novelty, and the rest of the meal. The dishes were all new to him, for Jenny had imposed her own way of cooking and of living on her staff. In this rainy little community cut off from the rest of India, founded mainly by the British for the British, they might have been in another world.

"If ever that palace in the south, with all the intrigue and difficulties of life down there, grows too much for you, you and Andhra must come and join us in Darjeeling," Mark said, lighting up his English briar pipe. "Tea bushes flourish naturally in this climate without too much effort, and when the railway is finished, communication with the rest of India will be very much easier."

"As a last resort, perhaps," Ranjana conceded. "I should feel out of my element here. The Summer Palace and estate came unexpectedly to me by the will of the gods, and I feel it is now up to me to transform and develop it to the best of my ability, for the good of the wretched coolies, in spite of all the opposition and setbacks. Andhra feels the same way. With a foot in each camp, so to speak, she understands and appreciates both worlds, but basic India, with its heat and dust, its mystery and misery, its splendor and squalor, is her true environment. I doubt if she would wish to leave it permanently."

Mark nodded agreement. "You are right, of course. India exerts a strange fascination on all who come into close contact with her. Even we Britishers succumb to it when we are enmeshed for any length of time. It was a wrench to change to more Western ways when Jenny and I first married and came up here. You and Andhra would feel it even more."

Ranjana retired early and was up and away at dawn. Whatever the outcome of this mission, he would return to Darjee-

ling to collect Ayah and little Sanjay and take them back to the
Summer Palace, he promised Jenny as he mounted his horse.

"Pray heaven you have Andhra with you," she called with a
catch in her voice.

He had no difficulty getting a passage upriver on a cargo
tramp steamer with a few passenger cabins when he reached
Calcutta. The accommodation was rough, but it mattered little
so long as he was on the move. To occupy his mind, he remained on deck with the captain while they negotiated the
treacherous reaches of the lower Hooghly River, in which so
many boats came to grief.

The skill of the navigator brought them safely to the broad
waters of the Ganges, thronged with river craft of all kinds,
from boatloads of pilgrims making for Benares to unwieldy
barges transporting rice, coal, coir and tea. It was a river full of
interest, yet Ranjana longed only for journey's end and was
glad to disembark at a small, squalid town and join an equally
squalid small steamer about to chug up a narrow tributary.

"I am going only a day's run and back," the owner explained.
"Where are you bound for?"

Ranjana mentioned the name of the convent, asking if it was
anywhere near the boat's destination.

Not very far away, he was informed, but he would have to
make a detour by road, as no boats went the entire distance.
The riverbed was rocky and the water turbulent.

He could walk it, he was told. There was a rough track that
climbed away from the river, then swung around to return to it
farther on, past the turbulent water.

"The convent is at the water's edge," he was told, "and the
kindly nuns always have a swarm of unwanted urchins over-
running their premises."

Just the kind of place Andhra might be induced to linger in
and help out, he reflected, especially if the old ayah had added
her pleas. Yet if this was the case, why had she not been in
touch with him or with Jenny?

It was a mystery he might soon solve, he thought as he left
the boat at sundown and turned his steps away from the river.

Darkness would soon fall, but with it would come the moon,
giving him enough light to pick out the track. He would tramp

all night if necessary, for how could he rest, now that he was so near.

He was saved such an effort, reaching the sprawling buildings before midnight. But the gates were shut and locked, and everything was quiet. It would be a mistake to try to rouse someone and demand admittance at this hour, he realized. They might well set the dogs on him, believing him to be a bandit, up to no good. He must wait for daylight.

He found a patch of dry grass sheltered by a sprawling banyan tree and curled up there, covering his head and face against night insects. Fatigue brought unconsciousness. He slept, oblivious of everything, unaware that Andhra had indeed passed this way but had now wandered far off with a troupe of homeless entertainers, bereft of all things past and almost as miserable as he in her wretched tent with a scheming old woman.

He was roused by the insistent call of a bell bird to find broad daylight about him. The sun was rising above the horizon. Soon the heat of the day would descend like a burden, now that he was far away from the Himalayas. He felt uncomfortable in his crumpled garments and longed for a ladle full of the refreshing cold water of Darjeeling to pour over his head, but only the arid landscape and dusty track met his gaze.

Neither was there the consolation of a cup of tea, but that at least could surely be obtained in the convent. He had money on his person, though he had left spare clothes with Jenny.

He rose, stretched and walked briskly to the gates of the convent. They were still locked, but a woman whose bare feet were deformed by leprosy was sweeping the courtyard beyond. At first she just stared suspiciously when he called for admittance. Then, at his insistence, she hobbled off, to return presently with a serene-faced young woman enveloped in snowy white.

"I am Sister Olive," she said. "What can I do for you?"

"I wish to talk to you, if you could let me inside," Ranjana said. "I have come a long way and waited all night, sleeping in the open."

The nun eyed him appraisingly. In spite of his disheveled appearance and the fact of his sleeping in the rough, he was clearly no dubious character. His rumpled garments were of excellent quality, his face as handsome and noble as a god's. Maybe he was in some deep trouble and needed guidance even though their religious beliefs were widely different.

"You must be in need of refreshment," she said quietly, taking a key from a bunch hanging at her waist and unlocking the gates. "Come inside and tell me what troubles you after you have eaten."

A pump stood in the middle of the yard. She indicated it, explaining, "We are fortunate to be so close to the river. The pump only runs dry in severe weather. After you have washed, join me in that office over there, where refreshment will be waiting."

Gratefully he walked to the pump and doused his head and face, then slipped off his sandals and cleaned his dusty feet. Now he felt able to face anything again, he reflected as he thrust them, still dripping wet, into his footwear. Towels were scarcely necessary in this climate and would certainly be a luxury in this poor community.

Tea was already waiting for him when he entered the office, and food, too, of a kind—a small quantity of cold cooked rice on a square of palm leaf.

"I'm afraid our fare may seem frugal to you," she said apologetically, "but the more carefully we ration supplies, the more unwanted waifs we are able to take in. Their need—and ours—is great."

This pittance probably represented a good meal to them, he realized with a pang, resolving to leave a generous donation when he departed.

The tea and rice consumed, he glanced at the nun, who sat mending worn saris for the children.

"Now you may tell me why you came," she murmured. "I am in charge here since our dear reverend mother went to her rest."

"I am hoping you can help me in tracing my wife," he said. "She started off on a train journey from Madras on a visit to her sister in Darjeeling. She never arrived there. Neither of us has heard any word from her, and naturally we are frantic with anxiety."

"What makes you think an obscure community such as this could know anything of her whereabouts, I wonder. We are hundreds of miles from the route you mention," she pointed out.

"True, but it seems possible she broke her journey at Calcutta to visit her old ayah, who is within your community, I understand."

"I see. We certainly gave shelter to a worthy old woman some years ago. She died recently at a ripe old age. I recall it vividly, because the circumstances were unusual. She was most eager to contact a young woman for whom she held a gift in trust. This woman did have connections with Darjeeling. I was so glad when she turned up just before old Ayah died, so that I could pass on the gift. Could that have been your wife, I wonder?"

"If she was young and beautiful as all the stars rolled into one, that was she!"

His ardor touched her heart, so that she longed to say, She is safe here with us. The truth was too disturbing: that weeks had elapsed since the incident occurred, and the visitor had left the same day and should have arrived in Darjeeling long before this. Yet it had to be told.

She saw the fear in his eyes.

"This gift," he said hoarsely. "Was it valuable?"

"Very, I should say. A small gold star encrusted with diamonds and rubies. Wisely, the woman concealed it in the folds of her sari, but . . ."

The unfinished sentence spoke volumes, conjuring visions of robbery, abduction, even murder. Ranjana bowed his head in his hands and prayed for strength and guidance. Then he rose, squaring his splendid shoulders.

"You have been as kind and as helpful as you could. It is noble work that you are doing here. Please take this offering as a token of my gratitude."

She stared at the large rupee note. "That is most generous of you," she said warmly. "I earnestly hope that your quest will reach a successful conclusion, and to that end I shall remember you in my prayers tonight. May God go with you and guide you. This gift will be a blessing here, rest assured."

What now, he wondered somberly as he left the convent behind. There seemed only one course open—to return to Darjeeling in the faint hope that somehow, whatever had intervened, he would this time find his beloved waiting there for him.

But first he must pay a brief visit to his brother, his nearest relative since the toll of the fateful mutiny. It was some years since they had met, and one day's delay in getting back to Darjeeling could matter little now, not after the passage of weeks.

So he trudged back to the river landing stage, scarcely glancing at the broken pieces of a wrecked bullock cart lying at the roadside and quite unconscious of the dramatic role it had played in the disappearance of Andhra.

An ancient steamer was about to sail downriver. He boarded it and sat under the tattered awning, watching the varied river life. The sun had now climbed high and was a force to be avoided when possible.

He left the steamer when it put into the next tiny port of call. Here he managed to hire a horse, which enabled him to take a short cut through a jungle trail. This at last brought him out on rising ground directly above Chandipur, where he reined in his mount and stood looking down on the place of his birth.

There was the palace just below him, looking much less imposing than he remembered it. The Summer Palace, his present home, set so beautifully on its placid lake in the far south, was much more attractive. Small wonder that Uncle Balbir coveted it so fanatically and seemed prepared to go to any lengths to wrest it from him.

Around the palace below clustered the crumbling town, with its pitiful hovels and small dark shops and, beyond, the bungalows of former British officers and officials, most of them now deserted ruins since the burning and looting following the mutiny. Beyond these rose the grim outlines of the fort, where Andhra and Jenny, along with all the other army families, had taken refuge from the carnage. Few of them had survived, but mercifully the two girls, along with Mark and a handful of others, had managed to make their escape against all the odds.

Pray heaven she would do so again, he reflected with fervor, if she was still alive and in any kind of danger.

With a grim expression he made his way down to the palace and rode in through the broken gateway. Evidence of neglect was clear enough now. The gardens and shrubberies, once so neat and bright with brilliant flowers everywhere, were withered and yellow. Only a small strip adjoining the dwelling looked as though it received attention and water.

His brother apparently was having a hard time running the place. Not for the first time Ranjana was glad that he had not been born the elder son, destined to carry on tradition in the face of all odds. He would never have been able to implement his ambitious schemes here.

His brother, Prince Vinita, was surprised but pleased to see him. "I was feeling bored," he confessed. "Now we can have dinner alone together while you tell me all your news. It will be good to get away from the squabbling women with their incessant demands."

Vinita evidently kept a harem, Ranjana reflected as he made his way to the bathroom to freshen himself after his journeying. Yet he was willing to wager that not one of them could compare with his own jewel, the incomparable Andhra. He wanted no one save her.

The bathroom was a mere cubbyhole with a stone floor and a drain in the middle. There was the usual round tub in which one stood to ladle oneself with water from a dipper and large pail. He stripped off his crumpled garments and doused himself liberally until his raven hair and entire body were dripping and deliciously cool, then rubbed himself vigorously with a towel, rather worn but kept meticulously clean by beating on river stones and bleaching in the sun.

Then he donned the clean attire brought to him by a servant, handing his own clothes over to be washed. "I shall need them tomorrow morning, as I'll be leaving then," he instructed.

"All shall be ready, Prince," he was assured.

The salon in which he and Vinita took their meal was as traditionally furnished as when he had lived here in his boyhood, with its silk hangings, fretted carvings, divans and cushions. Ranjana felt quite out of place sitting cross-legged on his worn cushion beside the low table. He much preferred the Western convenience of his own dining room, so disapproved of by his servants. It also irked him to have to eat his rice with his fingers again, an inelegant business involving many tiny bowls of flavoring sources. Why could not his brother adopt Western-style cutlery?

Inevitably they talked of the old days, when their way of life seemed set to drift along to the ends of time as it had always done. Who could then have foreseen the scale and depths of the horror about to burst upon them, in which their parents and sister had been swept away, along with much of their wealth and power.

"And you, my brother, how do you fare in your palace far in the south?" Vinita asked. "With your unconventional Western outlook and the sweeping changes you are determined on, things cannot be easy for you."

Ranjana smiled wryly. "You speak truly. The coolies are stupidly reluctant to change their way of life and refuse to believe that tea plantations can flourish there and bring them prosperity. Yet I'm sure they would have been less difficult but for Uncle Balbir. He has never forgiven me for inheriting what he always expected would come his way, and never will, I fear."

Vinita shrugged. "Why do you struggle against fate, with such a thorn in your flesh? Much better to be resigned to tradition and live as I do."

"But does it make you happy and fulfilled, I wonder? I ask more of life. I intend to leave conditions better in my small sphere of influence, if possible. That way lies satisfaction. I am fortunate in having married a Western-educated farsighted treasure whose outlook is the same as mine. Together we may realize our dream, if the gods relent."

"She is well, and your son? Why did you not bring them with you? I have not as yet seen either."

Ranjana's face clouded. Briefly he told Vinita the reason he came to be in the vicinity of Chandipur, and of his grave fears for Andhra.

"You are truly to be pitied, brother. I will do what I can and place an advertisement in our local journal, but I must admit that I consider your chance of finding her not good. How fortunate that she gave you a son before this strange disappearance. You can always take a concubine, as most of us do."

Such a remark was like a red flag to a bull. Ranjana's hands clenched, and it was an effort to remain civil. He was glad when he could retire with the excuse that he must be off early the following morning on his long journey to Darjeeling to collect his son.

Hope sustained him all the way. Surely Andhra would be there, waiting. But his hopes were cruelly dashed. Jenny had neither seen her nor heard any word.

So, sorrowfully, he and Mumtaz with little Sanjay were forced to return to the Summer Palace without her.

CHAPTER THIRTEEN

"We need rain badly. Lots of it," Robert Pearson declared as he and Ranjana strolled around the estate the following day.

There was no doubt of it. The land, apart from the neat plots of tea saplings, was growing parched and desertlike. But for constant attention and watering, they would have been the same.

"It makes a lot of extra work for the coolies, having to cart water out from the lake," Robert added. "A problem not usual in Darjeeling or in the uplands of Ceylon. I think we should seriously consider installing pumping machinery from Delhi to cut down on the labor and guard against possible drought."

Ranjana nodded. "Of course. The rainy seasons down here are different from the rest of India and cannot be relied on, I understand. They usually have two short, distinct periods, but monsoons can fail anywhere. We can't trust to luck, so we'll order the necessary machinery and pipes without delay. We're sure to be kept waiting."

It was an effort for him to raise any real enthusiasm. The baffling riddle of Andhra weighed too heavily upon him. As yet he could not steel himself to face the fact that he might never see her again. Life at the Summer Palace without her would be a hollow mockery. All the worthwhile plans they had dreamed up together would seem futile if she was not there to see the flowering with him.

At the heart of him, Robert was almost equally cast down. Andhra was the sun in his heaven, too, even though he dared not show it openly.

"Come and have a sundowner with me," Ranjana invited as he turned to walk back to the palace.

Robert hesitated. Without Andhra's illuminating presence,

the palace held no attraction. "I think I'll push on to my bungalow and try to get through regarding the pumping machinery, if you don't mind," he murmured. "The sooner the better, I think."

"As you please." Ranjana walked slowly down the hill. What was there to hurry for?

In the courtyard he subsided onto a cane lounge chair and was about to ring the bell for the house bearer when Rakhee glided up and squatted down beside him.

"What do you want?" His voice sounded flat and tired.

"I come to offer my sympathy, Prince, because you have returned without the princess. Also to warn you that Balbir Mukti is making the most of it. The bazaar in Cochpur is full of whispers that she has left you, never to return—gone off to some other lover, now that disapproval of her liaison with Robert Pearson is too strong."

His hands clenched. At that moment he wished savagely that they were around Balbir's skinny throat. Then a thought struck him. Could the villain have had anything to do with Andhra's disappearance? His influence was strong. He had spies and toadies everywhere, and nothing was too base or devilish for him to sink to. If he believed that this new trouble might drive his nephew away from the estate he himself coveted so fanatically, he was quite capable of having Andhra abducted, perhaps in teeming Calcutta where she was not known. And it would be simple to keep her a prisoner. Or perhaps she had been shadowed on her detour to the convent.

He passed on his suspicions to Rakhee, knowing that at heart she hated and feared the nawab and would have broken away from him had he not been so powerful. Therefore she would not betray his trust.

Rakhee frowned in deep thought. "As to abduction I cannot say, yet there is something in the air, I would swear. Only this very afternoon I came upon him deep in talk with one of his most villainous cronies, and now you mention it, I believe I did hear the word *abduction* pass between them before they realized my presence and broke off."

Ranjana's eyes flashed. The thought was enough to seal the old schemer's fate, and yet it brought renewed hope, suggesting as it did that Andhra was still alive and that he might yet gain her back. He must not let rage blind him but must use as much guile as Balbir himself did.

Rakhee looked apprehensive. "Do not make any hasty move, Prince," she cautioned. "If you accuse him point-blank of arranging the disappearance of the princess, he will guess that I have been in touch with you and perhaps beat me. He is a devil when displeased. Besides, it may not be true."

"I have no wish to make your life even harder," Ranjana declared. "It is a thousand pities you cannot break away from such a tyrant. You could live well enough by your dancing alone."

"That is true, wise Prince. Yet he declares that unless I base myself in the women's quarters of his palace, to be on hand whenever he wants me to dance for his guests—or for any other purpose—some frightful punishment will come my way. He is quite capable of maiming me so that I can no longer titillate and delight other men."

"You make me ashamed that I am forced to acknowledge him as my uncle." Ranjana touched her expressive hands, which had often transported him to magical spheres with their sensuous mime.

"Only one force could wrest me from his clutches," Rakhee murmured, seeing her advantage and pressing it home. "If some other man, almost equally powerful, were to take me under his protection, Balbir Mukti would be forced to leave me alone. Such a man as you, I mean."

Ranjana did not jump to the bait. At last he said decisively, "Perhaps I would welcome you had I been married to anyone save Andhra. She is a jewel beyond price. I need no woman save her. Neither would she tolerate it. So you must find some other escape from your irksome position. Remember, we are of the Western school of thought."

She knew when she was defeated, yet would he still be so adamant as time passed, if it brought no return of the woman he loved? A man's desires could not go unappeased forever.

But Rakhee was not entirely self-centered. Noting his sad dark eyes and the taut line of the mobile lips that she would have given anything to press her own upon, she genuinely hoped that the princess might turn up again so that this king among men would regain his customary spirits.

"It grieves me to see you so unhappy," she murmured. "I wish I could help you. I will listen and watch, back in Cochpur Palace. If I can find out anything, I will send a message to you. A young groom in the stables is madly in love with me and would do anything for me. He can ride this way on the pretext of exercising one of the horses, if it is impossible for me to come myself."

"That is kind of you. You are good as well as beautiful, and maybe the day will dawn when I can help you escape to a better life. I hope so. Now I shall have refreshment sent out to you before you return to Cochpur."

Ranjana's one comfort at this time was the fact that his little son was safe and well in his own home, with his devoted ayah to care for him. If the gods were unkind enough to decree that Andhra should never return, at least he had a part of her in their child. But he would not give up hope yet.

Ayah became even more protective of her precious charge, watching over him night and day, pushing him out for airings in his elegant perambulator every morning so as to keep him healthy and thriving for the day when his beautiful mother might be given back to him. Each night she prayed fervently to Siva and all the gods that this might be soon, and most mornings she turned the perambulator in the direction of the nearest small temple, taking some tiny offering to appease the gods.

She was returning one morning from such a mission, perspiring freely from her exertions in the heat and wishing that the monsoon would break to lay the choking dust. She had reached a deserted stretch of road that was closed in on either side by spreading banyan trees when, to her consternation, two men sprang out from the concealing growth. One seized her, the other, the baby. Without a word they were hustled into a waiting rickshaw and the pram was pushed out of sight behind the trees. One of the men jumped into the vehicle, tied a scarf tightly around Ayah's mouth to stop her screaming and another around her wrists. Then he flung a cotton cloth over her and the child, leaped out, seized the front shafts of the rickshaw and made off at a run, his companion pushing behind.

Little Sanjay whimpered in protest at this unusual treatment, but with Ayah still close beside him, he did not make too much fuss. In any case, there would have been no one to hear and rescue him. The two men trotted off down a near-deserted side track, meeting only an occasional coolie intent on his own business. The sight of a rickshaw bowling along was so common as to attract no attention whatsoever.

Ayah, sweating beneath the cotton cloth in mingled rage and fear, dared not struggle for fear of hurting Sanjay or even knocking him out of the swaying contraption. Being unable to speak soothingly to him on account of the gag, she was forced to sit docilely and listen to his whimpering, speculating on this new calamity and wondering if it had been engineered by the same source that had spirited away the princess. If so, they might possibly be taken to the same place. That was her only comfort.

After what seemed an interminable time, at the end of which she felt half suffocated by the gag and the concealing cloth, the rickshaw was set down with a jolt. The cloth was whisked away and the gag and hand binding removed, and she found herself in a desolate landscape quite unfamiliar to her. Set among dusty palm trees and wilting shrubs was a solitary thatched hut ringed by a bamboo fence. Her captors opened a gate and thrust Ayah, with Sanjay tightly clutched in her arms, through into a squalid compound that was overrun with skinny fowls and mangy goats. Patches of green and red peppers, melons and other vegetables waged a losing battle against heat and the onslaught of the livestock, while several naked urchins added the final touch of degradation.

Ayah recoiled in dismay. The *chota sahib* could not possibly live in such an atmosphere. Surely they were not to be kept here until a ransom had been paid. If so, she prayed that it might soon be forthcoming.

A woman in a bedraggled sari emerged from one of the two rooms of the hut. She spoke in a dialect not familiar to Ayah, then ushered her into the second room. It was almost empty of any amenities, but there was a pile of clean, fresh rice straw in the corner that would serve as bed and seats, a brass cooking pot and pitcher of water, and one or two other utensils.

The woman withdrew, leaving the door open, knowing that her prisoner could not escape. Not only was the bamboo fence too high, but a mangy yellow dog slunk around the compound, keeping a watchful eye on the strangers. Beyond the fence was only wilderness.

Back at the Summer Palace, no one noticed that Ayah and her charge had not returned from their morning walk until lunchtime. Then, while Ranjana was halfheartedly consuming his fish and soy sauce, a houseboy entered to report that they were not in the nursery as usual. Neither were they in the garden in the vicinity of the palace when the servant went out to look for them.

Ranjana set down his fork. It was unusual, to say the least, for Ayah to keep Sanjay out in the hottest part of the day, but there could be various explanations. She might have met a friend at the temple and be indulging in a prolonged gossip. Doings at the palace were always hot news, especially since Andhra's inexplicable disappearance. Or she could have grown tired from pushing the perambulator in the mounting heat, have found a shady retreat and be taking a rest, with Sanjay crawling contentedly around her. Whatever the explanation, there seemed no cause for alarm.

"I expect they will turn up quite soon," he said. "One doesn't grow hungry enough in this weather to drive one home, but keep their food in the kitchen for them."

Yet a faint unease compelled him to leave the new plantings early and return to the palace before his usual time, later that afternoon. He hastened up to the nursery, confident of hearing Ayah crooning one of her soothing Indian lullabies to calm her lively charge, and get him ready for sleep.

The silence that met him sent a distinct chill down his spine in spite of the heat. There was no sign of either in the self-contained suite.

He hastened downstairs to encounter the houseboy, who had now lost his Eastern calm.

"Ayah and the *chota sahib* have still not returned, Prince," he exclaimed with rolling eyes. "What can have happened to them? I fear some new calamity is about to afflict this troubled dwelling."

Ranjana's heart felt like lead. "You are sure that the gardens have been thoroughly searched?" he demanded.

The boy assured him that this had been done, then sidled away, afraid of the murderous glare in his master's eye.

But Ranjana's wrath was not for the wretched houseboy. He was recalling Rakhee's words—that she had fancied she had heard talk of abduction between Balbir and one of his most fanatical cronies. Had he mistakenly applied it to Andhra's disappearance, when in reality Balbir had been instigating the kidnapping of his little son?

Rage blinding him to everything save the need to confront his villainous uncle, Ranjana ordered his horse to be saddled and rode furiously out onto the dry track of the public road, leaving a yellow cloud of dust kicked up by his horse's hooves in his wake.

Hot, begrimed and weary, he presently arrived at Cochpur Palace to be greeted with suave reserve by the older man.

"It is not often that you condescend to pay me a visit, Nephew," he declared coolly. "To what do I owe this one?"

"You know very well, you old schemer! What have you done with my son?" Ranjana roared.

"Truly you speak in riddles," his uncle declared. "I have sons in plenty that my concubines have given me. Why should I covet the fruit of your loins?"

"To drive me frantic, surely, and force me to turn my back on this south land that is bedeviled by your machinations. First my wife, now my son! I warn you, Balbir, that if you harm either of them you shall pay for it with your life!"

Balbir's face flushed with anger. "Such threats I will not tolerate," he hissed through clenched teeth. "Take care you do not push me too far. You may be master of the Summer Palace, but in the rest of this district, I am more powerful than you, and my word is law. I know nothing of your wife, save that she brings your name to the dust by being the talk of the bazaars."

Ranjana's hands clenched. "My son, then. Do you deny any knowledge of his disappearance also?"

"Flatly and emphatically. Now get you gone from my house before worse than words fly between us."

From the corner of his eye, Ranjana caught a glimpse of a bright gold sari. Rakhee was hovering near. Perhaps she wanted to pass on some information she had gleaned. So without wasting any more time, he turned and stalked to where he had left his horse hitched in the courtyard.

The swift darkness had now almost fallen. He peered intently about but to his chagrin could see nothing of the girl. There was no other course than to ride out through the gate and hope desperately that Rakhee would send a groom out to the Summer Palace with some clue, as she had promised.

He did not have to wait long. Even as he rode slowly past a clump of hibiscus flanking the gates, from behind them emerged the gaudy form of the dancer.

"I dared not contact you in the courtyard," she whispered hurriedly. "Even here I may have been seen and followed. Go to the dwelling indicated on this paper. It may yield something; I cannot be sure. I have done my best for you, my prince."

With a great surge of gratitude in his heart, he leaned down and took the slip of paper from her pink-tipped hand. Then, impelled by the yearning in her piquant face, he leaned lower and pressed a kiss of thanks on her rounded cheek.

"Bless you!" he murmured before she glided away.

Not until he was well away from the palace did he pause and open the paper. In the fitful light cast by the lantern on a food vendor's stall, he read the few words it contained.

"Try the dwelling of Rahid Patur, near the village of Ootnapur." That was all, but it was enough to give Ranjana added strength to speed home like the wind.

Having never heard of Ootnapur, he sent for the houseboy, who was a local man. Ootnapur was about five miles away, he was informed, and the dwelling of Rahid Patur about a half-mile to the north, off on its own. Rahid Patur had been a farmer but was now dead, and his wife lived a meager existence on the rundown plot.

Just the kind of wretched creature Balbir's henchmen would pick on to do any dirty work for him, Ranjana realized. She would not dare to anger the nawab, however loath she was to hold prisoner a strange child and his ayah.

He conferred with Robert on the most effective way to raid the place.

"Since we cannot be certain little Sanjay is indeed being detained there, we had better proceed with stealth," Robert advised. "These small holdings always have several mangy dogs around that would attack us and raise the alarm if we tried to force our way in. Our best plan would be to go under cover of darkness, with some poisoned meat as bait. The dogs, being half starved, would wolf it down if it was dropped over the fence. When it had done its work, we could go in and investigate without too much trouble."

"That is sound advice," Ranjana agreed. "We will go tonight as soon as darkness falls."

So the two of them set off on horseback, carrying the poisoned meat and a rope scaling ladder to climb the inevitable fence.

They found the dwelling eventually and waited patiently until all sound of movement had ceased and the occupants had obviously retired. Then Ranjana dextrously threw the rope ladder over the high bamboo fence, making sure that it was firmly hitched on the uneven top. The more lithe of the two men, he then climbed nimbly up and dropped the meat over into the enclosed space, catching a glimpse of at least one mangy dog before he retreated.

The noise, though it was slight, brought the animal bounding up with a snarl. This was strangled in its throat as it caught the scent of the meat and began to gulp it down with slavering jaws.

The two men waited patiently and were presently rewarded with whimpers from behind the fence. They could picture the animal writhing in its death throes. Soon there was utter silence.

Ranjana mounted again. A glance over the top in the rising moonlight showed the dog lying motionless. He signaled to Robert that he was going over and climbed carefully down into the enclosure.

Beyond vegetable plots stood a thatched dwelling. He approached it with caution and peered in at the empty square that acted as a window. Several bodies lay asleep on scattered straw, quite oblivious of anything happening outside.

Satisfied that they were not the object of his raid, he passed on to the window of the second room. Here he dimly discerned a form in white cradling a small figure in its arms. His heart gave a leap of exultation as a whimper in the beloved voice of his son assured him that he had found his quarry.

Ayah, ever alert to the slightest sound from her charge, murmured a sleepy reassurance. Ranjana, not daring to take the risk of entering the doorway between the two windows, gave a sibilant murmur.

"Ayah, it is I, Prince Ranjana. Make no sound, but hand the baby through the window to me. Hurry, hurry!"

With a suppressed gasp Ayah struggled to her feet, the child clutched to her bosom. She thrust him into his father's arms, then, realizing she could not climb through the window without noise, flitted like a shadow to the unlocked door and out to join the prince.

"Come," he murmured, making for the fence.

A soft word to the invisible Robert brought him up the outside ladder to peer over the top. Ranjana mounted inside and passed over the sleeping child.

"Lay him down and come back to help Ayah," he instructed. "She is not as nimble as we are."

Soon all four of them were safely outside. Ranjana mounted his horse, clutched Sanjay in front of him and rode off. Robert swung Ayah up on his own horse and followed.

Back at the Summer Palace, Ayah told the story of the abduction. Though now surer than ever that Balbir was behind it, Ranjana realized that nothing could be proved against him. No one dared give away the all-powerful nawab for fear of their lives, so it was useless to probe further at the lonely farm or make any other inquiries.

All Ranjana could do was forbid Ayah to leave the palace grounds and so expose his son to further danger. Ayah, in fervent agreement, declared that nothing would induce her to venture forth again. In future she would be content to push the perambulator of the *chota sahib* only around the garden paths.

"Now all I want is my beautiful Andhra," Ranjana confided to Robert the following day. "If only I could discover her whereabouts and rescue her, too, I should be the happiest man alive."

Privately Robert was beginning to relinquish all hope of this. He doubted very much that Balbir was responsible for her disappearance, too. It seemed more likely that she had been killed or abducted in the far north for the value of the jewel she had received at the convent, and that they would never see her again.

Yet he kept his fears to himself, knowing that Ranjana had enough troubles with the deepening drought and the uncooperative attitude of the coolies.

Ranjana was pleased to run into Rakhee while he was in the bazaar to make some purchases the next morning. He thanked her sincerely for enabling him to rescue Sanjay, adding, "For the love of all the gods, keep on the alert for any scrap of conversation that could give a clue to Andhra's hiding place. I still think my evil uncle may know more of her disappearance than he admits to."

Rakhee looked doubtful. "I do not think he is involved there, my prince. Nevertheless, I shall watch and listen for your sake."

"If you succeed, you can ask anything of me," he declared with low intensity.

"Anything?"

"Even to the extent of my protection to get you away from your hated master."

Her eyes kindled. To be the prince's concubine she would cheerfully commit murder, but the task of finding his wife was likely to be more difficult than that. Yet she only said, "If it is possible, it shall be done. For you I would sell my soul to all the demons in mythology."

Comforted a little, he returned to the Summer Palace, there to be confronted by a miracle the wonder of which he had never known. A wise old man had traveled down from the north with the most astounding news and was waiting to pour it all out. Not only was his darling Andhra safe, but she was a noble-born princess, now under the protection of her illustrious father in the palace where she had been born.

"She is well and fit?" Ranjana gasped. "Then why did she not contact me before this, knowing how much I would be grieving for her?"

"Nay, Prince, do not blame her. She has been suffering from total loss of memory and still recalls little of her past life. We are hoping that the sight of you will restore her to normal again."

Almost beside himself with joy, Ranjana left the estate in Robert's care and set off yet again, this time on a most welcome journey.

CHAPTER FOURTEEN

A week had passed. Under the loving care of Mira and the skilled treatment of Vishvonathan, Andhra was a different person. All her glowing vitality and sparkling health had returned. Dressed in the most costly of silk saris, her lustrous hair oiled, braided and piled into a becoming crown, she looked every inch a maharaja's daughter and the princess that she was by birth.

Her injured ankle was responding well. She could now take short walks around the palace and the extensive gardens.

Her father and Vishvonathan had been busy on mysterious telegraph calls, among other things. They both exuded an air of expectant excitement that set her hopes soaring, but they would say nothing definite beyond, "All in good time, my child. We have a definite reason for keeping you in the dark at the moment."

"If all turns out as we hope, the shock may be just the factor needed to bring back her lost memory," Andhra overheard Vishvonathan remark to her father one morning. "This afternoon we shall see."

Acute excitement gripped her, especially when, as soon as lunch was over, Mira dressed her with more than usual care.

"You're a magician!" Andhra said as she gazed at her alluring reflection in the long mirror. "You've given me the breathless charm of a bride awaiting her groom."

Mira nodded, displaying her toothless grin. "And maybe that is just what it will turn out to be," she said with the air of a conspirator, gazing fondly at her new idol. With her softly voluptuous figure sheathed in a gauzy sari of misty pale blue spangled with silvery flowers, Andhra might have stepped straight down from one of the arresting pictures adorning the walls.

Was he coming—the elusive prince who haunted her dreams, whose touch shattered conventions, leaving her drowning in a deep warm sea of ecstatic desire.

"Soon, soon," Mira promised. "Come to the salon to await him in fitting style."

She would say no more but led her charge into the large and splendid apartment where the maharaja sat among the cushions in splendor, as eager as she to see the outcome of his negotiations.

It seemed an age before Vishvonathan glided in, saying deferentially, "He is come, master."

"Then show him in."

The servant murmured a word or two outside the door and discreetly retired, while in through the portal strode a splendid young Hindu. Tall, lithe, with an arresting olive face and magnificently attired, he would have stood out in any company. Here he blended perfectly with this sumptuous room of the Randevi Palace, proclaiming his own high-born heritage.

As his gaze fell on Andhra there was a moment's stunned silence, while many emotions flashed over his mobile countenance. Then, with a strangled cry of "Andhra, my wife!" he strode across the luxurious carpet without even a glance at the maharaja and folded her in arms desperate for her.

A blinding flash of recollection seared through Andhra's clouded mind, bringing the most poignant joy she had ever known. This was he who had haunted her dreams, too elusive to be named or even seen clearly. This was he whose passion could rouse her own emotions to ecstasy almost beyond endurance, until shattering climax brought fulfillment that left her warmly spent in his arms. This was her beloved, her prince, her husband.

"Ranjana," she murmured wonderingly, savoring the name that had eluded her these past months, scarcely daring to believe that he was real and not merely the phantom that had tantalized her to tears when she lay desolate and lost beside the old mother of the traveling entertainers.

He soon proved he was no phantom. As the maharaja moved quietly from the room, well pleased with the success of his scheme, Ranjana was covering her beautiful face with kisses so passionate that they brought pain as well as joy. It mattered not at all. She wanted them to go on and on, longed to be kissed and caressed all over, with seeking, searing lips and hands that left her innermost being bruised, burning and gloriously alive.

"My pearl, my lovely one," he murmured hoarsely. "How I have longed and agonized for you. How I cursed the gods when you just disappeared into limbo on that ill-fated journey to your sister in Darjeeling. I still cannot imagine what happened, and why you came to be involved with strolling players, as your father informs me you were. The very thought turns me cold with horror. It is a miracle that you survived such trials unharmed. You must tell me everything presently, but first I must have you all to myself and know again the joy of union. Only then shall I realize that the sweetest being in all the world is no longer lost but mine again, to love and hold."

"Come, my prince." As eager as he, she led him toward her bedroom, and it was then that she remembered little Sanjay.

"My baby!" she entreated. "Where is he? Is he well?"

"Do not fret, dear one. Sanjay is in the best of health, lovingly cared for by Mumtaz. They await you in the Summer Palace, far away in the south."

He shed his splendid clothes, revealing the bronze, virile form that she knew so well. She slipped off her own sari and stood naked before him in all her golden beauty. A veritable god and goddess, they might have stepped down from the erotic carvings on one of the Hindu temples.

Fulfillment was as magical and ecstatic as they had dreamed of. Afterward, when they lay with arms entwined, the shadowy past came flooding back in full. She was able to recall why she had left Calcutta on a secret mission instead of going straight to Darjeeling.

"For your sake, my prince, I wanted to find out who I was by birth, and I felt that my old ayah was the only person who could help. She passed on this jewel I wear, the Star of Randevi, but died before she could tell me more. Then an accident to a bullock cart in which I rode left me concussed, my memory gone. The traveling entertainers found me, and you know the rest."

He nodded, clutching her tighter, as though afraid she would be torn from him again.

"I can imagine what you went through," she murmured feelingly. "And yet I think the end will justify the means." She held up the jewel that hung around her neck, its rubies and diamonds twinkling in the subdued light.

"This proves I am of the royal house of Randevi, the daughter of a maharaja and a fitting bride for you, my prince. No longer will your uncle be able to point a finger of scorn at me and say I am not fit to rule with you and be the mother of your sons."

He laughed with satisfaction. "It mattered little to me who your father was, my pearl. But for the sake of our son and your own peace of mind, I am glad that all has come to light and my miserable Uncle Balbir stands confounded."

"How is the estate progressing, dear one?" she asked. "I seem to have been absent for an age. Some of the transplants must be in production now."

A shadow crossed his face. "You have not heard, I suppose, of the failure of the monsoon in the south? For some reason the rains largely passed us by this autumn, and on the western *ghats* and the surrounding land there is a serious problem building up."

She frowned in concern, seeing in her mind's eye the tropical jungles and lush growth of the deep south. "Perhaps they'll come later, my prince, as they so often have a winter monsoon in addition to the summer rains."

"I pray so, along with many others. Already cattle are starving and dying in remote rural areas. Rice planted at the traditional season is withering and dying, and unless we get those heavy late rains, famine, with all its horrors, will stalk the land. We've seen the effects of that so often in the northeast. It happens so seldom in the south that the coolies just don't know how to face it, while the authorities are not in the least geared to deal with it. They're just living in hope of the rain coming later."

"What of our estate at the Summer Palace? Fortunately we

have the lake surrounding us." She was acutely aware that young tea saplings needed water every day if they were to survive in the heat of the south.

"True, we have the lake. But remember it lies in the valley, while the tea plantations are on the higher hill slopes, the most favorable position for their development. Getting the water up to them is proving extremely difficult, and it is impossible to keep them all watered daily as they should be. I'm afraid we're bound to lose some of the saplings, just as they were making such good headway."

Andhra clicked her tongue in concern.

"I can just imagine how Uncle Balbir is gloating and saying it serves me right for starting tea plantings in the deep south, where they have never before been grown. Even the coolies are muttering that tea is only for the western foothills of the Himalayas or the cool moist uplands of Ceylon—behind my back, of course. I'm praying that the gods will not prove them right, or I'll stand condemned in my own eyes for grubbing up their wretched little plots and forcing them to work with tea."

"Wretched little plots is just what they were!" she said stoutly. "They must have frequently starved when relying on what could be grown under those circumstances, so you mustn't blame yourself, Ranjana. You acted in their best interests as well as your own. It's just very bad luck that the rains are failing this year in the region where the monsoon is usually predictably heavy. My first task on my return to the palace will be to go to the temple and pray for rain."

He smiled ruefully. "I'm doing something a little more positive than that, my love. I sent to Delhi for some machinery to pump the water from the lake up to where it is needed. But you know how slowly things work in this tradition-bound land of ours. When it will arrive at the Summer Palace I cannot say. Quite possibly too late."

She looked concerned. "It sounds bad!"

"It is—very bad—but we may yet survive if the gods relent and send the rains quickly."

"My thanks to them that we're together again at last," she said fervently. "Life must have been well nigh insupportable for you lately with so many worries."

He nodded. "But now that I have you safely back, we shall face things together with hope and courage, my love. Tomorrow we must set off. It was unfortunate that I had to leave the estate at this critical juncture, but nothing would have kept me from coming to fetch you when your father contacted me with news of your miraculous appearance."

"He's going to be unhappy when he hears I must leave him tomorrow." She sighed. "I believe he had visions of keeping me for the rest of his life, lonely old man that he is."

It was indeed a blow to him when he heard next morning of Andhra's imminent departure. "Why not come and make your home here in the Randevi Palace with me?" he begged. "It would be wonderful to have you and my grandson and your favorite servants. You could do as you pleased. And of course everything I possess will pass to Andhra on my death, she being my true daughter, the sole child of my late wife and myself."

As gently as he could, Ranjana thanked him but pointed out that they had their own palace and estate waiting for them, with a great new venture at stake.

"If the plantations succeed, I shall have done something for the impoverished south that will go down in history," he explained. "They desperately need new industries, however much they fight against it in their tradition-bound way. The only factor that might defeat me is the weather. I cannot control the elements, unfortunately."

"You must come and visit us, my father, whenever you feel so inclined," Andhra urged. "The steam trains make travel easy down to Madras, and there you would be met."

"One day I shall," he promised. "And of course you in turn must look upon this palace as a second home. There will always be a welcome for you here."

It was not until they were comfortably seated in a first-class carriage, speeding home, that Andhra remembered Robert Pearson, the English plantation manager.

"Robert must be as concerned as you over the impending drought," she said.

"He is. He has never had to contend with a water shortage

before, having always worked in cool, damp Darjeeling. He was desperately trying to organize relays of water carriers before I left, but the coolies are sullen and uncooperative. Their own small plots around their new living quarters are parched, their crops withering. Instead of blaming the gods as usual for any misfortune, this time they blame me. My uncle is still behind them, secretly fanning their discontent, I fear. Now you see why I am so eager to get back to the estate, my love."

She nodded, then, going off at a tangent, asked, "Have you seen much of Rakhee during my absence?"

He laughed. "I know what you mean. Why not come straight out with it? In spite of her disappointment on the occasions our paths did cross, I never made love to her, for the simple reason that I was too devastated by your disappearance. I could think of no other woman in that light at that time."

She pressed his hand. "Thank you, my prince."

"And you, my pearl? What of this musician and snake charmer whose life you shared? It is inconceivable that neither of them cast lustful eyes upon your beauty. Did you manage to keep them at arm's length? If not, I will seek them out and kill them as I would a poisonous snake in the jungle."

"As the gods are my witness, have no fear, my husband. It was as you supposed. They did indeed desire me. In fact, the mother kept pressing me to marry her son. I refused all advances. Fundamentally, I knew that somewhere I had a godlike man of my own, who made all others seem like slimy toads."

His answer was a passionate kiss in the privacy of their first-class carriage.

Signs of imminent drought became evident as they neared Madras. The cattle, always thin, were now so emaciated that their ribs seemed on the point of bursting through their taut skins. Rice paddies that should have been bright green with thriving crops now presented a sickly yellowish appearance. Coolies, ragged and gaunt, worked spasmodically, trying to stave off the inevitable. Naked children played silently and listlessly, while hollow-eyed women competed with water buffaloes for the sluggish trickles of water flowing through the drying mud of what as this time of year should have been full rivers.

Sick at heart, Andhra averted her gaze as the train passed slowly through the blighted landscape. How many of these people would die unless the gods relented and the rains came swiftly?

Madras looked more normal. Cities were the last to be affected in such a situation, but privation would follow when the wells ran dry and water was cut off.

It was good to see the rugged, deeply tanned face of Robert Pearson waiting at the station. Andhra noted with concern his air of anxiety. No doubt the weather situation must be telling more heavily on him than even on Ranjana, being directly responsible for the running and welfare of the new plantation and its workers as he was.

His expression lightened when he greeted her. She remembered that he had been in love with her and still was. It was there in his eyes.

"How are things?" Ranjana asked tersely.

"Worsening. I just hope that pumping gear reaches us quickly from Delhi."

Ranjana's mouth hardened, but the set of his splendid shoulders revealed that his fighting spirit was unimpaired.

The carriage ride was a long one, winding up into the hills, but they reached the Summer Palace at last in late afternoon. It looked as serenely beautiful as ever, surrounded by the shimmering waters of the lake. But as they passed over the bridge connecting it to the estate, Andhra could not fail to see that the water level was much lower than when she had last seen it. Even the palace gardens were wilting, she noted.

"I'm sorry, but I was forced to set the gardeners helping out with carrying water for the sapling tea plants," Robert apologized. "Even so, I'm losing more every day. I'm desperately worried, and see disaster unless that pumping gear arrives soon."

"I'll get on to the railway authorities without delay," Ranjana said grimly. "It must be lying neglected on some siding. Corruption and red tape are all too prevalent in the despised south, we know to our cost. But even allowing for that, it should be at Madras by now."

While he went about this business, Andhra made her way eagerly up to the nursery, her heart beating faster at the thought of seeing her son again.

She gasped at the chubby little bundle staggering uncertainly from one vantage point to the next in the blue and white nursery. Seeing her, he stood stock still, his dark brown eyes fixed upon her in puzzled wonder.

With a strangled cry Andhra swooped upon him, gathered him up in eager arms and showered kisses on his golden face and black curls.

"How you've grown, my baby," she murmured at last, tears starting for the lost months when she had missed the small achievements of babyhood.

Although by now she was almost a stranger, he did not cry but smiled in delight, thrusting his fingers through her glossy hair.

Ayah came forward, grinning broadly. "Welcome home, my mistress. The *chota sahib* has not quite forgotten you. That is good."

Andhra sat with him on her lap, intensely happy to feel the warm weight of him again, unable to tear herself away.

"It is his bedtime soon. Maybe you like to undress him," Ayah suggested with tolerant understanding.

Andhra stayed until he was in his white cot, shrouded by the mosquito net, then hurried back to see if Ranjana had gained any satisfaction from his inquiries.

She found him sitting tight-lipped in the spacious salon.

"Sabotage!" he said tersely. "While the truck was on a siding overnight, only ten miles from Madras, somebody tore off the tarpaulin and stole the lighter pieces of machinery. The rest was scattered over the track along with the pipes. They'll be sending it on, but it will be quite useless without those vital parts."

"Oh, no!" She looked stunned. "Who do you suppose it was?"

"I have a good idea, after breaking the news to Robert, who stayed to learn when we could expect the pumps and pipes.

Now, of course, we're back where we started, with no mechanical help whatever."

"What light did he throw on the vandalism?"

"Why, he caught Shukur Thayar, the rascally manager we had to dismiss, hobnobbing with the coolies one day, picking up what gossip he could from them. They would doubtless mention the expected machinery, which he would promptly relay to Uncle Balbir. My worthy uncle, who was no doubt gloating over the prospect of drought ruining the tea plantation before it had even started production, must have decided to put a wrench in the works and prevent any usable pumps from ever reaching us. He no doubt found out just where the truck was and sent a bunch of toadies to do their worst. He has plenty of influence, you know. In fact, he rules the entire district."

Andhra pressed his hand in sympathy. "Are we never to be free of his animosity, my prince?"

"It appears not, until the gods strike him down."

"And in the meantime we face disaster unless the rains come."

He clenched his hands. "We'll move heaven and earth to stave it off, Robert and I, by rallying the coolies. He has gone to tell them they can expect no help from machinery yet, and we'll have to salvage what we can by our own efforts. It won't be easy. They're in a sullen mood, he says. Understandably, perhaps, with their own new vegetable plots withered and livestock dying. In their superstitious ignorance they're laying the blame on me, saying I've angered the gods by flouting tradition, plowing up the estate and planting a crop never before grown here."

Andhra clicked her tongue impatiently. Having been educated in England, she fully shared Ranjana's thirst for progress and his wish to benefit this poverty-stricken south by proving that profitable tea could be grown. At the same time, she understood the coolies' fears.

"We must go among them ourselves tomorrow morning," she decided. "Perhaps I can influence some of the women at least and make them realize this is a natural disaster, with the whole of the south suffering."

He nodded, but his expression showed no optimism.

They set off immediately after breakfast the following morning to cross the bridge and climb the slopes. Ayah insisted on going part of the way with them, desirous of showing off the handsome little pony cart Ranjana had bought for his son. Little Sanjay, laughing with glee, sat strapped into the single seat, brandishing a miniature whip. Ayah walked alongside, keeping a guiding hand on the reins to steer the docile little gray pony.

Andhra could not share her son's pleasure. She was too sickened by the sight of the seedlings, which had been green and healthy when she had last seen them, now sickly and yellowing in their parched beds. The transplant cuttings, brought originally from Darjeeling, were in an even poorer state of health, not having the tap roots of the seedlings to search for moisture.

"Being used to the cool, moist climate of the foothills of the Himalayas, they won't stand these conditions for long," Ranjana said grimly.

"Where are all the coolies? Why aren't they working?" Andhra wondered, glancing around her to see only the odd figure, head swathed against the sun, listlessly poking at the dusty, dry soil with primitive implements.

"Why indeed! Here comes Robert, looking pretty grim. No doubt he'll enlighten us."

Striding down from the new longhouses of the coolies, his expression was indeed murderous. "Three quarters of them have fled in the night, the miserable skunks!" he explained. "Deserted us like rats leaving a sinking ship. Now we haven't a hope of survival. Come and see for yourself."

Ranjana and Andhra followed as he turned back up the slope, while Ayah, tired of walking uphill, faced the pony for home.

The long huts, thatched with palm leaf and rice straw, and the two-roomed family dwellings, presented a strangely silent air when they were reached. They were usually hives of activity and cheerful sounds, with wives singing as they thrashed maize and rice in the garden plots, and children playing noisily. Now the pestles and mortars were gone, the plots as arid as

a desert, the grunting piglets eaten and the skinny fowls transported.

As they stood rooted in dismay, a frightened face peered
from one of the huts.

"I'll see what's behind it all," Andhra called, hurrying forward to speak to the woman in her own language.

Five minutes later she was back. "Uncle Balbir again! We
might have known. He sent Shukur Thayar yesterday while
you were away meeting us, Robert, to tell the coolies that the
pumping machinery would never arrive. The estate was
doomed, for this year at least, and unless they wanted to die of
famine, they had better make an immediate move. He promised help to get them all transported from Madras to Ceylon in
a ship owned by one of his friends, so they packed their bundles and set off at sundown with wives and families to trek to
Madras. Only a handful stayed behind—not nearly enough to
pull us through this crisis."

They stood in stunned silence for several moments. Then
Robert squared his shoulders. "We won't give up without a
fight!" he ground out. "We'll have to let half the plots on these
highest slopes go and save what we can of the lower ones.
There are a number of water carriers lying around. We'll collect them and put our few remaining coolies to work."

"There are two in the palace gardens for a start," Andhra
recalled. "But it will be hard work pushing full loads of water
uphill, won't it?" The water carriers were like dustbins on
wheels.

"Of course. We'll put two men to each carrier. We could also
utilize the oxen that we purchased for plowing the land.
They're slow and ponderous, but strong."

"Bless you, Robert, for being so enthusiastic in the face of
disaster!" Andhra said with feeling. "Thank the gods for the
lake. I just hope it doesn't dry up."

While Ranjana and Robert set about rounding up coolies and
carriers, Andhra hurried back to the palace, eager to take up
the reins again. After such an interval it would be strange
giving orders to the cook again, and rupees for shopping in the
bazaar. Surely he would now show more respect after

Ranjana's announcement at breakfast of her royal origins, and perhaps his cooking would improve.

But first she went up to her room to sponge her face and change her sari, for the climb in the heat plus the agitation brought on by this latest crisis had drenched her in perspiration.

But another shock awaited her. No sooner had she closed the bedroom door behind her than out from the capacious cupboard that housed her extensive wardrobe of saris stepped Rakhee the dancer.

For a moment Andhra stared in disbelief. Then anger took over. "What on earth are *you* doing in the palace, and hiding here of all places! How dare you?"

Then the devastating suspicion crossed her mind. Was Ranjana deceiving her?

Rakhee's black eyes flashed. "I know what you are thinking, Princess, but it is not so. Prince Ranjana was quite uncorruptible during your absence, in spite of all my wiles. He has no idea that I am here now. I have only just come and hidden myself in here until I could speak privately with you."

Andhra bit her lip. "Go ahead, then, but it had better be quite genuine, for if I find you are trying some trick, I'm quite capable of losing my temper and having you thrown out."

The dancing girl now threw herself dramatically at Andhra's sandaled feet. "Oh, Princess, hide me! Save me from that vile old lecher Balbir Mukti and his equally vile son," she begged.

This was totally unexpected and entirely in accord with Andhra's own opinion of Ranjana's uncle. Besides, on peering more closely, she noted that Rakhee looked genuinely scared, hollow-eyed and peaky, in marked contrast to her usual sultry attraction.

She pulled the girl to her feet, motioned her to a brocaded stool, and sat on the bed to listen. "Now tell me what has happened. You were quite happy to satisfy Balbir's lust and take his money formerly. What has changed you?"

"His demands grow more and more vicious, Princess, and his son is as bad. They take aphrodisiacs and drugs that make them insatiable, and leave me too exhausted to dance well. My art is suffering, and soon I shall no longer be the queen of the dancers. No one will want to hire me."

"Is there nowhere else you can go to get away from them?"

"Nowhere. They would soon find me. Here it is safe. They would never think I would be here now that you are back."

"How long would I have to connive in this deception?"

"A week only, until they have given up seeking me. Then I will slip away and maybe go to Madras. I could easily make a living there."

"The servants here would find out and talk."

"Not if I remain hidden up here all the time. Please, please say that you will help to save me from a fate that has become unendurable."

Sympathy and a desire to protect another woman rose within Andhra's breast. This hunted creature was quite a different proposition from the seductive wanton flaunting her charms before an enthralled Ranjana. She seemed genuinely scared, and with good reason, for Balbir, nawab of Cochpur, was a powerful ruler, and dancing girls had little status in the scheme of things, depending chiefly on men like him.

"I'll help you," she conceded at last, half reluctantly. "Fortunately for you, there are few servants left in the palace. Ranjana sent them packing when he overheard a group of them calling me vile names during the months I was missing. We still have a cook and one or two bearers, but Ayah waits on herself and the baby and cleans her own nursery, where she washes Sanjay's clothes and bathes him. She can bring up a little extra food for you when she brings up her own meals from the kitchen."

"She will not gossip to the cook?"

"Not if I forbid it. Mumtaz is the most loyal of servants."

So a bedding roll was installed and Ayah's help enlisted. At first she pursed her lips at the notion of waiting on a dancing girl, but when she learned that it would be only for a week, and moreover that it would foil the villainous Balbir's designs, she consented with as good a grace as possible.

With some reserve Andhra told Ranjana of the arrangement. It was undoubtedly flinging temptation his way, yet she had never felt more sure of his love and loyalty. In any case, all his thoughts and energy were now directed on the doomed estate. If even a fraction of the saplings were to be saved, the few coolies left must work like demons under his tireless leadership.

CHAPTER FIFTEEN

Another week of drought came and went. Day after day the sun beat pitilessly down from the brassy sky, making their already difficult life well nigh unendurable. The entire countryside was now parched and brown as a desert. Every morning the wretched inhabitants trudged for miles to the nearest river, to compete with men, women, children and animals for the ever-dwindling supply of precious water in the drying mud beds. Most rivers were now a mere trickle, and bloated, dead carcasses of water buffalo, oxen and dogs scattered the dusty ground, the pitiful result of lack of food and water.

It would soon be the turn of human beings. Famine stalked the land, for inevitably no water meant no food. Fear stared out from the gaunt faces and hollow eyes of the poor. They knew from experience that governing bodies were slow to act and road conditions atrocious. Any help finally sent by corrupt authorities would arrive too late to save many of them.

Things were a little better at the Summer Palace. They had the lake for general use of water and a deep well in the grounds for precious drinking water. There was also a good stock of rice and other staple foods in the storeroom off the kitchen, but the fate of the new tea estate, planted with such high hopes, was grim. Three quarters of the higher land was now as devastated as any to be found outside. By leaving it to its fate and concentrating on the lower beds what water they could transport by the small carriers, they had managed to keep a proportion green and fairly healthy, but the waters of the lake were dwindling alarmingly with these unusual demands.

Andhra was glad of the narrow bridge, the only link with the mainland. A guard with rifle and ammunition had been posted there to keep at bay any bands of desperadoes who might be driven to attack the palace in search of food. Andhra longed with all her heart to share what food and water they had with those less fortunate, but as Ranjana pointed out, the unfortunates were so numerous that if they began handing out alms they would soon be overwhelmed, the palace reserves exhausted, and they themselves facing famine. For little Sanjay's sake if not their own, they must hold out as long as possible.

"I would feel happier if you, he and Ayah were far away from this trouble, with your newfound father," he said somberly. "The drought only afflicts the south."

"That is something I refuse to consider," she said stoutly. "We have been parted long enough, my prince. We shall weather the storm together or go under together."

"May the gods forbid that it should come to that, my pearl. But these are grave times for the south. The sleeping tiger of India is awake and rampant, and only the gods can vanquish him by sending those elusive rains."

It was true, Andhra realized, striving to quell the fear within her. Only that morning the cook had mentioned fears of tribal uprisings if the government did not act quickly. Half the population of one remote village had starved to death, he had heard in the market, and the remaining coolies had looted a grain train that had been on its way to alleviate the situation.

"The hill tribes must be in an ugly mood," Ranjana went on. "The highest land around here has no reserves of water; the roads are mere dust tracks and they are remote from railways or government help. We are most vulnerable from some of those. The Kerbul tribe poses the biggest threat. They are half civilized at the best of times, living from hand to mouth with their goats and stony land. Pray heaven they do not descend on us. Their scimitars are deadly, even though they own no guns."

For the sake of safety and convenience, Robert had now moved into the palace, leaving his new bungalow high in the withered plantation. The few remaining coolies still slept in their huts with their families, coming down each morning to work on the lower beds of saplings.

Now Andhra was glad that they were so few and that only a handful of staff were left in the palace. They made less demands on the dwindling supplies of food and water. The food had to be watched carefully and doled out by her with caution, for the local market had ceased functioning. There were no fresh vegetables or fruit for the coolies' wives to bring in for sale, no meat because poultry and livestock were dying of hunger. Stores of grain were exhausted or jealously hidden by any who were fortunate enough to possess them, and altogether the outlook was bleak in the extreme.

"How your Uncle Balbir must be gloating," Andhra remarked one morning as she, Robert and Ranjana were eating a meager breakfast. "The drought has done his dirty work for him—effectively ruined the plantation for some time at least."

"Luck seems to be favoring the old reprobate," Robert said grimly. "I heard yesterday when I was in the village that he has Rakhee back in his clutches. His minions caught her soon after she left here, before she could get away to Madras."

"And he certainly will not be suffering through the drought," Ranjana said tersely. "His storeroom will be stocked with commodities that should have gone to the most stricken villages."

"One day," Andhra murmured, "his sins will rebound on him. The gods have all-seeing eyes and long memories."

The two men had not long left for the lower plantation and Andhra was surveying the lake, now alarmingly low, when across the bridge came one of their coolies. He explained that his wife was very sick with the shivering sickness and he had no medicine to give her. One of the other wives was with her, but he feared she might be beyond hope by the time he reached home that evening.

Shivering sickness. Malaria, undoubtedly, Andhra reflected. The woman needed quinine, and quickly. That, and keeping her warm during the alternate shivering and sweating, was the only remedy possible.

"You go to your work among the saplings, and I'll go up with medicine and a cooling drink for her," she promised.

He went off with profuse thanks, and Andhra gave orders for her horse to be saddled, as riding would be faster and less fatiguing than walking. Then she collected what she needed, placed the things in her saddlebag and set off.

Only her horse and Ranjana's remained in the stables, and soon they would have to be sacrificed, she reflected grimly. They ate and drank too much, and their flesh would make a great many meals for starving people. The thought was repugnant but had to be faced. Much more revolting things than horseflesh were being consumed these days.

She reached the coolie hut. The woman lay glassy eyed, with chattering teeth, muttering in delirium. Andhra forced the correct dose of quinine between the cracked lips with the help of the woman attendant, gave the latter instructions, heaped what coverings she could find on the heaving form and left. There was nothing else she could do, and in these troubled times she wanted to be back in the safety of the palace as soon as possible.

The ride back downhill would be easy and exhilarating, she reflected. She could give the horse his head. There was no one to gape at the spectacle of a princess galloping indecorously on horseback, minus riding habit, with sari flapping in the breeze.

But a shock was in store. Scarcely out of sight and hearing of the coolie huts, another horse and rider came cantering across the ruined plantation to draw up squarely in front of her. A dart of fear passed through Andhra as she surveyed the rider's sinewy form. He was sunburned almost black, and naked except for a filthy *dhoti* around his loins. The bearded face beneath the turban was gaunt and fierce, the eyes as piercingly cruel as a hawk's. The hands grasping the reins of his emaciated horse looked capable of murder, and the gleaming scimitar dangling by his side gave point to the view.

This, she realized with sinking heart, could only be one of the Kerbul tribe Ranjana had mentioned that morning. Grown desperate because of the drought and knowing that most of the coolies had deserted the plantation, he had swooped down to comb the higher reaches in search of anything of value.

"So, my fine princess," he said mockingly in his own language, which Andhra barely understood, "you do not look as though you are suffering like the rest of us. It is time you shared your possessions with those less fortunate."

She remained silent, horribly conscious of her vulnerability. He looked quite capable of snatching her horse's reins and dragging both it and herself back to his stronghold as ransom hostages or, worse still, hurling her to the ground and raping her in the most revolting manner.

His laugh was scornful. "Never fear, Princess. If I so much as touched you, your precious husband would be in honor bound to pursue me to the death. I fear no man under equal terms, but he possesses a gun and is a deadly shot, I have heard, while I have only my trusty scimitar. What else have you to give?"

She rallied the courage she had always possessed. "Nothing to you! If any of your women or children are ill or starving, I will try to send aid up to them, but even the palace resources are running short now."

"But not your jewels, it seems." His hawklike eyes were on the Star of Randevi, which had slipped into view during her exertions. As proof of her high birth, she wore it continually, and it had become one of her greatest treasures.

"Hand it over, and your bracelets, too. Food is scarce but can still be bought at a price in the right quarter."

"The bracelets you may have, but not the pendant." She calmly removed the gold and silver circles from around her wrists and held them out, preferring this to him taking them by force. He was no doubt the chief of the hill tribe, ruthless, strong and desperate in the face of the present calamity. She was in no position to argue with him.

He took the bracelets in his left hand. As she bent toward him, his right hand shot out, grasped the pendant and wrenched it savagely from her neck.

"This will keep my people from starvation for some time!"

"Oh no! Take my horse if you like, but leave me my birth star," she protested.

"The horse is of no use at this time. We cannot feed the ones we have. They'll be slaughtered for food before long."

With a mocking smile he raised his hand in salute, then, turning, galloped off uphill toward the parched jungle.

She had to bite her lower lip hard to hold back tears of mortification and rage. After having been deprived of the beautiful pendant for most of her life, it was hard to have it snatched from her again. What would Ranjana do when he

heard of the encounter? The conjecture filled her with fore-
boding. He was not the man to let such an outrage pass.

All pleasure in the canter downhill had evaporated. The
drought-devastated land alone was enough to alarm the
stoutest heart, without the knowledge that in their isolated
position, they were no longer safe from starving and desperate
hill tribes.

Only the lower tea beds looked thriving, with the handful of
coolies toiling to keep them going. Robert and Ranjana worked
as hard as any of the hands, driven on by the determination to
save at least a nucleus of the estate they had conceived with
such enthusiasm.

There was Ranjana now, his clothes soiled and wet with his
exertions. Hearing her horse's hooves on the iron-hard path, he
came toward her.

"I hope you have not been far afield, my love. It is hardly safe
to ride alone in these troubled times, even on our own estate."

Then, noting the distress on her lovely face, he added,
"Something has happened!"

"One of the coolies' wives had a bad case of malaria. He
asked for help this morning, so I went up with medicines,
knowing no one else could be spared. Just as I was setting back,
a fierce-looking fellow on horseback confronted me—apparently the head man of that Kerbul tribe you mentioned this
morning."

"Go on," he said tensely.

"He said they were starving and demanded my jewelry to
buy food on the black market. I passed over my bracelets—I
had no choice, really—but he wanted more. When I refused to
hand over the Star of Randevi, he snatched it from my neck
and galloped off."

Ranjana's hands clenched. He looked as though he were
about to explode. "He'll pay for this!" he said savagely.

Apprehension flooded through Andhra. "What can you do
against a desperate tribe, my prince? You alone?"

"Stealth must be used, of course. A surprise attack while he
sleeps. I know the settlement slightly, having ridden through it
when I was searching for you. The head man has a larger hut in

the center of the enclosure, which is in a depression farther up the hillside."

She grasped his arm. "Much as the loss grieves me, you know I'd a thousand times rather never see it again than lose you. Without you life is a desert."

"Courage, my love," he rallied. "I intend to kill, not be killed, and to snatch back your treasure before he can dispose of it. Therefore I must go tonight."

Sensing that something was amiss, Robert now strolled over from where he had been working. Ranjana briefly gave him the gist of the robbery.

He, too, was incensed. "Count me in on this!" he declared. "Two of us should stand a better chance than one."

This was some small comfort to Andhra. Thanking him, she glimpsed for a moment the naked love in his eyes and knew that he would count his life well lost for her.

Yet apprehension lay heavily upon her for the remainder of the day, so that she could neither eat nor rest. Mumtaz, with her wise perception, was confided in and put on a brave front in spite of her inner fears.

It was useless to retire to bed, Andhra realized after the two men had set off at sundown on their horses, armed with guns and daggers. Their plan was to ride as close to the settlement as possible, tether their horses, then creep to the chief's hut and search for Andhra's jewelry. If it could be found without rousing the man, they would take it and leave as silently as they came. If not, Ranjana would force him at knife point to reveal where he had hidden it, then either kill or gag and bind him until they made their escape. The guns would only be used as a last resort, because of rousing the rest of the tribesmen.

It sounded easy enough, but Andhra knew that events seldom worked out as planned. So many things could go wrong.

Faithful Mumtaz glided in with a tray of tea around dawn. "I knew you would be awake and anxious, my princess," she murmured, setting it down on a small table near Andhra's bed, where her mistress sat fully dressed, "so I went to the kitchen and made it myself. With so few servants left, I must do things I once thought beneath me."

"I know, Mumtaz. Someday, in better times, I shall make it

up to you with a whole string of silver bracelets to jangle on your wrists."

Right now there was no cash to spare for such luxuries. The estate had been neglected and rundown when Ranjana took over, and anything he could scrape together since had gone to laying out the new estate, erecting functional outbuildings and paying wages to the coolies. Now it was all threatened.

With broad daylight came greater anxiety. Surely the two men should have returned by now. Their mission could only have succeeded under cover of darkness, so what could be detaining them?

One thing only, she realized with sinking heart. Capture.

It was sheer torture to wander around the palace waiting as the sun rose higher, but there was nothing else she could do. Ranjana and Robert had taken the only two horses left in the stables, and it was both exhausting and dangerous in the present state of unrest to wander up the hillside alone, in the hope of sighting anything. To take her mind off the crisis, she played with little Sanjay in the garden until they both grew too hot, then sauntered to the bridge, where the sentry stood guard.

"You've heard or seen nothing of the prince or Mr. Pearson?" she asked.

He shook his head. "Nothing, Princess."

She was just about to go dispiritedly back to the garden when the whinnying of a horse alerted them both. A great rush of hope surged through her as she stared toward the hill, only to be followed by the most bitter disappointment. For into sight rode one horseman only: Robert.

She darted across the bridge and ran toward him. "Ranjana —what has happened to him?" she gasped.

"They've captured him," he said in a spent voice. "A prowling cur started barking and gave us away just as we reached the chief's hut. We were overwhelmed immediately, before we had a real chance of using our guns. I guess they half expected us getting on their tracks to retrieve the jewels and were lying in wait."

"Yet *you* managed to escape?"

"Not a hope. They sent me back for ransom guns and money,

and only because I fell afoul of one of their scimitars so am no longer a menace. I can't fight back."

It was then that she noticed his right arm hanging slackly by his side, with blood staining the sleeve of his shirt. He had guided his horse downhill with his left hand only.

"Oh, Robert, is it very bad?"

"I'll weather it, but it needs attention."

"Come quickly. I'll help you myself, since there's no one else."

Together they went inside, where she bathed and bandaged an ugly cut on his forearm. "It should really be stitched, but for that you'd have to go to the village doctor," she said.

"I'll have to take my chances on its mending without," he said grimly. "At the moment Ranjana comes first. They won't release him until I take as many guns and as much money as I can scrape up. We might run to half a dozen guns, but Ranjana says I won't find much ready money. He's given me authority to take what there is and get back as quickly as possible. He's worried about leaving you, Sanjay and the palace with so few to guard you in case they try some further treachery."

Together they rounded up what guns were available after Andhra had selected a pistol for her own protection. She was a fair shot at close range. Vividly at this time of danger her thoughts winged back to another time of turbulence, the Indian Mutiny, when her coolness and courage had saved the lives of her adoptive sister Jenny and herself. She could do as much again if the need arose.

The rupees in Ranjana's desk were not very numerous.

"Do you think, with the guns, this will suffice to release him?" she asked anxiously.

"We can only hope so."

Sensing his doubt, she burst out, "Surely some force of law and order exists in Cochpur! Couldn't a band be organized to go up to the tribe and force his release?"

"My dear Andhra," he said with a sigh. "You know the corruption that exists in Cochpur. The smashing of our water-pumping machinery in transit proves that. That old viper Uncle Balbir, nawab of the district, has a finger in every pie. Nothing happens without his authority. Can you see him sending a force to rescue Ranjana from the clutches of a half wild hill tribe? He'd be overjoyed if they killed him and only little Sanjay stood between him and this Summer Palace estate."

Her hands clenched. "I'm afraid you're right. Come, I'll find some refreshment for you, and then, hard though it seems, you must get off again. Rest is what you really need. You look quite exhausted. Why can't we send the guard up with the guns and money, the one reliable man we have left?"

"Because they specified me, knowing that at the moment I can't fight back. They warned that if anyone else accompanied me they'd knife us both on sight. They're a desperate lot and in deadly earnest because they're literally starving, like many others in this terrible drought."

He quickly ate two of the chapatties she brought, drank deeply of the now-murky well water and then set off again. It would be a grueling uphill ride, she guessed, weak and fatigued as he was from loss of blood, but there was no other way.

It was now lunchtime, but she could eat nothing. Mumtaz coaxed her into drinking some tea into which she had slipped a mild sedative, so that Andhra eventually slept for the rest of the day and through most of the night.

Morning came, with no sign of either Ranjana or Robert. "It is too early to expect them yet," Mumtaz said soothingly. "Lunchtime will bring them, maybe."

It brought nothing except further trouble. A group of villagers, driven to violence by the lack of water and the knowledge that there still remained some water in the lake, attacked and disarmed the sentry, stormed across the bridge, filled their water pots and jugs and marched off, shouting that they had more need of it than a few sickly tea plants. The few remaining estate coolies ran back to their huts, afraid to tend the plants any longer in case the villagers turned on them.

"So this is the end of all our hopes," Andhra murmured sorrowfully, surveying the devastated plantation, with the last few beds now left to go the way of the others.

But the plight of Ranjana and Robert was more urgent than any estate. It appeared that what Robert had taken by way of ransom had not been enough to satisfy the chief, and there were no more rupees in the palace. Any other assets Ranjana possessed would be in safekeeping in the Madras Bank, too unobtainable to be of use now.

Who could help, she wondered desperately. No one save Balbir the all-powerful.

Yet even had she possessed anything with which to bribe him, she doubted if he would use his authority to save Ranjana. He coveted the estate too much.

The estate! That was the only thing that might save her husband. If she went herself to Balbir and swore that she would use every weapon in her power to persuade Ranjana to turn the Summer Palace over to his uncle and go back to the north where he was born, then Balbir might act to secure his and Robert's release.

The thought of facing Balbir in his own palace, begging for help, was irksome in the extreme, but against Ranjana's life, it was a small price to pay. And with the Summer Palace as stake, surely his avarice would clinch matters and induce him to help her.

There was no time to be lost. She must ride on horseback to Cochpur. But where would she find a horse in these desperate times?

Prafull Anbad, the horse dealer, sprang to mind. He lived in the village and bred good-class horses to sell to the wealthy as polo ponies. Perhaps he had been forced to reduce his stables, but he would surely hang onto some of his stock, knowing that the drought must end sooner or later.

She put on her least showy sari, tied a gauzy scarf firmly around her head and hurried down to the horse dealer's. The pistol concealed beneath the muslin draperies gave her courage, and the small ivory elephant with ruby eyes that she carried gave her confidence that Anbad would lend her one of his horses. He had greatly admired it on a business call to the palace, so it would make acceptable security.

She found him looking unusually dejected, with most of his stock disposed of.

"These cruel times will be the ruination of us all," he said dolefully. "How can the authorities expect us to hold out without help?"

But he took the beautiful little carving, realizing that it

would keep its value always and not expire on him for want of food and water. In return he saddled and bridled his strongest remaining horse after hearing of her desperate need, and voiced his hope that the prince would be set free soon.

Andhra spared neither herself nor her mount. Fortunately the way to Cochpur was a gentle slope downhill. She arrived at Cochpur Palace at sundown tired, perspiring and dusty but with courage undiminished after her ride through the parched landscape.

Uncle Balbir's crafty face was inscrutable when she was shown into his private salon, but a triumphant gleam lit his black eyes for a moment as they rested on Andhra's seductive curves where the gauzy material clung damply to breasts and thighs.

"So, at last the proud one has turned humbly to the despised uncle with a plea for his help," he said as though enjoying the situation.

"Unfortunately I'm forced to, and since with your network of spies you'll know just why, it relieves me of telling you the whole story," she said stiffly.

"Now what makes you certain I shall intervene in this matter, after the bad blood between us, Princess?"

"Because you covet the Summer Palace and its land. You always have."

"True, but with Ranjana restored to it, I shall be as far from owning it as ever. What inducement could you give to make me act against myself?"

"Hopefully, the palace and land itself. The whole venture is ending in total disaster, due to one adverse circumstance after another. I for one shall be glad to leave it!" she exclaimed passionately. "If you use your influence to make the Kerbul tribe release Ranjana and Robert, I in turn will use mine to get Ranjana to turn the estate over to you and go back to the northwest, where tea plantations flourish."

He was silent for several minutes, so that her hopes died within her. With his face a mask, she could not follow the devious scheme running slimily through his mind like sludge through a sewer. At last he smiled thinly. "My dear princess, there is only one bribe high enough to induce me to save that interloping nephew of mine."

"What is that?" A hint of what he was thinking made her voice falter.

"You. I have always wanted you, the more so because you were so obviously out of reach. Give yourself to me tonight, and an order shall be sent tomorrow commanding the release of the two men. Material aid will be given to the Kerbuls if they comply, but a force of guns sent to blast them if they don't. Now what is your answer?"

She looked stricken. "How can I fulfill such a condition? And even if I did, you must know what the consequences would be for you. Ranjana would never rest until he had avenged me with your life."

"Just so, but of course you would swear not to tell him. It would be a secret between us. That would be part of the bargain."

What could she say? Never, never, never, and so probably condemn the two men who meant most to her to death? What would life mean to her without Ranjana? Nothing.

For Ranjana's life, a brief hour of loathsome submission was not too high a price for her to pay, surely. She *must* pay it, or live forever with regret.

He saw the struggle within her, realized that it could only end in his favor if he gave her enough rope, and said suavely, "You need time to think it over, and you are hot and tired from your long ride. I must go out to the courtroom for a while, to pass sentence on coolies caught looting a grain store. There is a room adjoining this where you can rest and refresh yourself. No servant will trouble you if I lock the door. Afterward you will have dinner with me and spend the night. Then I shall repay you by giving you an order of release for the two men, sealed with my official seal."

Andhra's hands clenched until her rose-tinted nails bit into her soft palms. For Ranjana's sake, she must say nothing and appear to agree. If she could induce him to sign the order first, maybe the dreaded ordeal could be avoided somehow. The thought of the pistol hidden beneath her sari gave her some comfort, until she realized that to use it would mean certain death for herself. The palace staff would be alerted by the report and prevent her escape.

There seemed to be no way out but the one from which she cringed.

CHAPTER SIXTEEN

Uncle Balbir unlocked a door hidden by a rich velvet curtain and opened it.

"You are honored, Princess. Only my most favored concubines ever reach this room. At present Rakhee enjoys that distinction, but her allure begins to wear thin. You may not find her company to your taste, but it will be for only a brief time."

He propelled Andhra into the room and locked the door behind her.

It was small but comfortable, with a cushioned divan, crimson carpet and hangings, a stand with fruit and drink. On the divan crouched Rakhee, her dark eyes too large for the hollow cheeks that had once been rounded with golden charm.

"I am sorry to see you in such a plight, Princess," she said in a low voice. "I listened at the wall and heard all that was said. Once I might have gloated at your downfall, but not now. Balbir is a fiend and I would gladly dance on his coffin. Besides, you were kind and hid me from him once, but he ensnared me again."

"I'm truly sorry for that," Andhra murmured, sitting down beside her.

Rakhee shrugged. "Forget me for now. Prince Ranjana is the one who matters. He whom we both love."

Andhra's lips hardened.

"Do not be angry, Princess. He will never betray you with me. I know. I tried hard enough once. He loves only you. As for me, my base desires have faded now. I love him as an exalted king, a god. He is a man of pure gold, far above me. I would gladly lay down my life if it would save his. This change has been wrought by that fiend Balbir, with his lust and drugs, so different from Prince Ranjana."

"He's gone to the courtroom, so we are alone for a while, unless his son Satish is in the palace."

"No. He went to the House of Pleasure, where dancing girls, drink and gambling will keep him occupied all night."

"Then we have a little time, if only we could think of some way out of this nightmare. I have a pistol," Andhra went on, "and wouldn't hesitate to use it on a skunk like Balbir if it would do any good. But even if I managed to extract a release order for Ranjana from him first, I should never escape alive from the palace with it if a pistol went off."

Rakhee shook her head. "No, we must be more subtle than that. Wheedle the release order from him by any means in your power as soon as you can, and I will try to help you escape."

Andhra turned a troubled gaze upon her. "Do you mean to imply that even if I gave in to him, he wouldn't honor his word and let me go to seek Ranjana's freedom?"

The dancing girl's laugh was mirthless. "What honor has a snake? He will rub his hands with glee if the prince is eliminated. That way he would hope to get both the Summer Palace and you into his clutches. He would never risk your husband finding out how you had managed to secure his release, so signing his own death warrant."

She was right, Andhra realized. Uncle Balbir was capable of any deceit and any crime to further his own ends. Whatever sacrifice she made would be in vain. Ranjana would be left to his fate at the hands of the Kerbuls. They would kill both Robert and him, so that they could return without opposition to the Summer Palace and take what they wanted.

She grasped Rakhee's hand. "You are my only hope, although I don't see what you can do against such a powerful man."

"For Prince Ranjana, I would do anything, risk anything," Rakhee said with absolute conviction. "I have a small store of drugs hidden away that I managed to filch a few grains at a time from Balbir's hoard when he was in a drugged stupor. I intended them to end my life if it grew too intolerable. Now perhaps they will save the prince's."

Andhra blanched. "You mean . . ."

"Ask no questions, Princess. Just trust me and behave normally when Balbir returns. But it is vital that you get a written order for your husband's release before the end of dinner. I shall let it be known among the servants here that you came solely to ask the nawab's help in releasing the prince. You must go at daybreak, on the plea that there is no time to be lost in getting the release order to the hill tribes."

"What of you? How can I leave you alone here in misery and danger?" Andhra asked.

"There shall be no danger if I am subtle. That is why I must stay. To flee would be to proclaim guilt, even if I escaped the servants' vigil. Afterward, if Balbir is no more, my chance will come. Satish has not so much power."

Andhra was forced to leave it at that. Rakhee was eager to clear away all traces of her long, dusty journey and make her look her best.

"You are never less than beautiful, Princess, but I can make you look so alluring that he can withhold nothing from you," she said.

She undressed Andhra, washed her in scented water, dressed her in a shimmering sari, made up her eyes with kohl so that they looked as large and mysterious as the Indian night, tinted her lips and cheeks, and braided her blue-black hair into a shimmering crown on the top of her head, entwined with fragrant frangipani. Then she stood back and clapped her hands.

"What man could resist you! No wonder the prince is so deeply in love with you. Balbir will drool over you, but remember, it is vital to coax that order from him as soon as you possibly can."

Soon after they heard Balbir moving in the adjoining salon. His commanding voice gave orders to deferential servants.

"They will be bringing dinner," Rakhee explained. "He often has it in private when he is not entertaining. Usually I have it with him."

Presently he flung open the door between and stood regarding Andhra with sensual delight. "Truly a pearl of great price," he said throatily. "Why, you make even Rakhee, the most alluring dancer in these parts, look tarnished. Tonight I shall be as one with the gods."

Andhra laid her hand caressingly on his arm. "You speak truly when you mention great price, my dear uncle. You know my price, so please be gracious enough to pay it first," she said in her most wheedling tones.

He shrugged. "Oh, that. It can wait until morning, surely."

She shook her head and playfully stroked his cheek. "Like you, I am accustomed to having my own way. Come, write the order now, and then we can both forget it and think of nothing save pleasure."

Her face was as guileless as a child's, yet at first he seemed about to refuse. But when she brushed his face with her soft lips, he smiled in spite of himself.

"Verily you are a witch. So be it, if it will make you more agreeable to me."

"And Rakhee may dine with us?" she asked as they passed into the salon and he found paper and a quill pen. It was essential to have her there, with her deadly potion.

"If you wish it so, though I thought you were deadly rivals. Well, why not? It will add spice to my food to have the two of you dandling around me. And after, you and I have all night to get to know each other better."

Andhra heaved a silent sigh of relief. Without Rakhee's aid the prospect of the night ahead would have been appalling. There was not even the comfort of her pistol upon her, for she had been forced to leave it in the next room with her own sari.

The meal was sumptuous: many small, exotic dishes set out on a low table, around which were piled rainbow-hued cushions. On these they sat, while stringed instruments strummed monotonous music somewhere out of sight. Coffee, tea and other drinks stood on a side table, from which Rakhee helped them from time to time, having dismissed the bearer.

"We need no servants at a love feast," she had said laughingly to Balbir. "I shall wait on my lord and master and put him in the best of moods, for tomorrow night the princess will be gone and he will turn to me again."

Balbir grinned. "Truly you have much merit, my dusky

dancer, and can please me well enough when you set out to do so."

So the scene was set for high drama. Andhra exerted all her skill to act naturally and let Balbir believe she was actually warming to him, though when his skinny hand fondled her breast, it took all her resolution to remain smiling. Only one thing restrained her from slapping his face, and that was the folded paper nestling in the hollow of her bosom—the vital order for Ranjana's release, signed and embellished with his signature and seal.

At last, sated with food, the nawab belched noisily. "Enough. To bed, I say, before I grow too sleepy to make the most of this unexpected delight flung upon me," he said.

Andhra's heart seemed to turn over. Had Rakhee yet added her secret potion to one of the cups she had handed him? If so, it had made no visible difference in him.

But Rakhee had evidently used all her guile, letting the man they both had cause to hate stuff himself with food and drink until his palate was too debauched to taste anything, for now she sprang to her feet and moved to the side table.

"One last really strong cup of coffee, my master, for that is best calculated to keep you awake until the bell bird sounds his morning call."

Balbir leered. "Bring two. I expect the princess to show me all the tricks she practices on that stallion of a nephew of mine to keep him drooling for more. And put a measure of aphrodisiac in each," he roared.

Rakhee poured and mixed, her movements hidden from view. For one ghastly moment the fleeting thought crossed Andhra's mind that it would be so easy for the dancer to fix both cups and so eliminate her as well. That way there would be some hope of Ranjana turning to her in his loneliness.

Andhra pushed the suspicion away as unworthy. In any case, there was nothing to be done except trust Rakhee. She was already returning, a cup in each hand. One she carefully handed to Balbir, the other to Andhra.

"Drink it quickly!" she exclaimed, laughing, "and then I shall make you a nest of cushions on which to enjoy your lovemaking."

Balbir raised the cup to his lips, gulped the contents down noisily and threw down the cup. Andhra took a sip from her own. It tasted of nothing save strong coffee.

"Drink!" he urged, "before I pour it down your pretty throat."

She finished the coffee, her attention all on Balbir. How long would the stuff take to work? With various mixes it ought to be twice as quick.

"We must clear the food and dishes before I can make things nice for you," Rakhee said, ringing for the bearer.

He came promptly.

"Be quick and begone!" his master ordered.

The bearer stacked food on his tray and pattered out on bare feet. He would be returning for cups, plates, coffee and tea-pots, and to push aside the low round table. Nervously Andhra glanced at Balbir. How long would the potion take to work? It would be disastrous if anything startling happened to the na-wab before they were alone.

It seemed an age before the servant came back. He gathered up the remains of the meal, carried the table to the side of the room and prepared to leave.

"Does my master require anything more?" he asked in def-erential tones. "Pineapple juice, or fruit, maybe."

"Nothing. Get out and stay out. I want nothing more to-night."

A tingle of anticipation shot through Andhra. Surely the potion and aphrodisiac were beginning to work. Balbir's voice was distinctly slurred, as though his tongue clove to the roof of his mouth. Thank heaven the bearer was leaving and seemed to notice nothing. She breathed a sigh of relief when the door closed behind him.

Rakhee began to arrange the pile of cushions to make a soft bed on the luxurious carpet as slowly as she could.

The nawab rose unsteadily to his feet, clutching his head. "Hurry, woman. Truly you move at a snail's pace. I must have indulged too freely with the curried prawns, for I feel most alarmingly odd. Maybe if I lie down quickly I will feel better."

His voice was even more slurred. He almost fell into the waiting nest, and lay staring up with glassy eyes.

"Come, lie beside me," he commanded, raising his hand toward Andhra. But the power of the drugs was having such an effect that it fell back as though useless.

Cringing inwardly, she complied. A few brief moments should see the end of the ordeal, by the look of things.

She had scarcely settled before he clutched his heart, grunting and gasping in a most violent way.

"I am ill! Send for a physician," he moaned, and now his voice was a mere croak that held no threat.

Rakhee bent solicitously over him, playing for time. "To be sure, my lord. But first is there nothing that I can do for you?"

Unable to stand the warm bulk of his body against hers, the fetid stench of his breath gusting into her face any longer, Andhra stumbled to her feet.

"Perhaps the bearer left some water," she murmured, glancing around.

The old reprobate was past water or anything else. He tried to speak, but only a whisper came. Then violent convulsions overtook him, racking his frame. His head and eyes rolled grotesquely, so that she had to turn away, covering her eyes to shut out the horror.

Presently Rakhee was beside her, laying a comforting hand on her arm. "It is finished. Do not waste pity on him, Princess. He would gladly have left Ranjana to be killed by the hill tribe and have used you the way he used me, until your life became intolerable. Besides, he has had so many helpless people whipped, tortured or killed for very little reason. Truly, the world will be well rid of him."

She was right, of course. This was no time for weak sentiment. They were now both in too precarious a position for that and must bring courage and ingenuity to bear to find the best way to extricate themselves before the early light of day disclosed the sensation to the world.

CHAPTER SEVENTEEN

"Courage, Princess. We have but a little time before day-break. We must think and discuss, so that our stories are identical when we are questioned," Rakhee declared decisively.

"I must get away, then," Andhra said with a shuddering glance toward the still form on the cushions.

"Of course." Rakhee drew her away into the smaller room she herself used, closing the door between.

"It will be quite natural for you to ride off at daybreak, letting it be known that you came here solely to obtain the order for Ranjana's release from the only man with authority over all people in this district. You were forced to stay over-night because it would have been dangerous for a woman to ride on horseback through the dark in these troubled times. The servants know that their master entertained us both at dinner in his suite, but that is all. Your story must go that you slept in this room afterward, while I remained with him in his salon."

"But how will you account for his death?" Andhra asked.

"I shall say that after making love he felt ill. He put it down to an overdose of aphrodisiac and other drugs he had taken, and sent me into this room with you while he slept it off. It is well known that he takes these things, so no one will be surprised. We shall both say we slept soundly and heard nothing. You will say that you rose at dawn and rode off without awakening him, eager to get that release order to the hill tribe before they harmed your husband. I shall remain in here, pretending to be sleeping, until the nawab's servant comes in with his tea as usual. He will raise the alarm, and I shall simulate shock and grief. They will assume that his liberal use of drugs and stimulants took effect at last and he died of a seizure."

Andhra nodded. "It sounds logical, but too easy. I wish you didn't have to stay here."

"I must. For me to flee just now would point suspicion and seal my fate. Do not fear for me. I shall weather the storm and go as soon as I can. I shall go to Madras, the big city beyond the reach of the power of this family."

They huddled on the couch together, too keyed up to sleep, speaking only in whispers. Andhra was infinitely glad when the early dawn showed gray through the small window and she could at last be away from this grisly place.

She washed, dressed in her own sari, made sure that both her pistol and the precious release order were concealed on her person, took a deep drink of water from a carafe, and clasped Rakhee's hands. "You have been a true friend. I shall pray with all my heart that you get safely away to Madras," she whispered earnestly.

"And I in turn shall pray that you reach the Kerbul tribe in time to save the prince from harm, or the palace from one of their raids. May the gods bless you both, and your little son."

On impulse Andhra embraced her, then murmured, "Is there any way out without having to go through the next room?"

Rakhee nodded and drew her to a low covered door. This she unlocked, and with a final whispered farewell, Andhra stooped and passed through the small exit into the early-morning freshness of a quiet courtyard.

"Go straight ahead," Rakhee murmured, pointing. "Turn left through the archway and you'll find yourself in the stable area. Even this early, some boy will be around to saddle your horse. Explain that you were too anxious to be away and effect Prince Ranjana's release to bother waking a servant and send out the order. They know you and your strange foreign ways, so there will be no comment."

Andhra nodded, pressed the dancer's hand once again and walked quickly away on sandaled feet.

She found a boy curled up in his bedroll outside the stable door. He rubbed sleepy eyes and made her horse ready with the dexterity of one accustomed to blows if he fumbled.

Soon she was mounted and riding through the front gates of

the palace, opened for her by a surprised gatekeeper, who nevertheless recognized her as a princess, wife of Prince Ranjana, nephew of his illustrious master, and bowed deeply in respect, hands deferentially clasped before his face.

How good it was to be free of that fateful place. She breathed in great gulps of clean fresh air, as yet unsullied by dust. Now she could let all her thoughts fly to Ranjana and Robert, and inevitably anxiety crept in.

Would she be in time to save them from harm? The Kerbuls must know of the dissension between Ranjana and his uncle and were doubtless counting on that to save them from reprisals for taking the two men prisoner and demanding a ransom. But when she presented a direct order for their release, signed and sealed by the nawab himself, the chief would not dare to disobey that.

Then a disturbing thought struck her. If the tribe by some mischance heard of the nawab's sudden death, would that make a difference? Would the chief feel he was not bound to fulfill the dictates of a dead man and keep his two prisoners until a ransom was paid?

With this in mind she was more anxious than ever to reach the Kerbuls before any hint of this latest sensation penetrated to them. Their isolation was to her advantage. It was unlikely that luck would run out just yet.

The ride back, being uphill, took a little longer than yesterday, but the morning air being fresher and the horse rested after his night in the stables, she was back at the Summer Palace by lunchtime.

A sigh escaped her as her glance took in the devastated plantation. The saplings withered, the ground baked hard. And what an ominous quiet hung over the entire place. It seemed utterly deserted.

She fastened her horse in a shady place near the veranda and hurried inside. A hush hung over the palace, too. It might have been a mausoleum.

Fear crept over her. Had there been a raid? Had anything happened to Mumtaz and little Sanjay? Frantic at the thought, she raced upstairs, arriving at the nursery suite out of breath.

The door was locked. She beat on it with her fists. "Mumtaz, are you there? It is I, the princess!"

A key was turned, the door flung open, and there was Ayah looking thoroughly scared, little Sanjay clinging to her sari.

"The gods be praised that you are back safely, my princess. But to what a welcome! The Kerbuls raided us yesterday afternoon, and the few servants fled in terror. Sanjay and I alone are left. We stayed quietly up here locked in, and I believe they thought the palace was deserted."

Andhra's lips compressed. "What did they take?"

"Food, Princess. That which is more precious than gold at this time of famine. After they rode away with their loot, I went down to see what was left. They had made straight for the kitchens and storeroom and left them bare. Sacks of rice and maize, dal, tea, dried fish—all gone. As though an army of locusts had passed over the palace."

This was devastating. "How are we to survive?" she whispered.

Mumtaz patted her arm with a consoling gesture. "Verily, Ayah is as cunning as they, Princess. After you had gone yesterday, I feared that with the master and Pearson sahib held prisoner and the palace unguarded, they would come hunting for food, so I outwitted them. Little by little I carried what I could from the storeroom and hid it up here. There is enough basic food to last a week or more for the few of us who are left. We shall not starve."

Tears started to Andhra's eyes. Mumtaz was a treasure beyond price. But there was no time to be lost, with Ranjana and Robert still to be freed. Hastily she passed on the news of what had happened in the Cochpur Palace, and of what still lay before her.

Mumtaz looked stricken. "You cannot go up into that den of bandits alone, and who is to go with you? Not one man is left. They fled before the raiders."

Andhra smiled grimly. "You don't know me, Ayah. For Ranjana I would do anything. I have my pistol hidden on me and can use it if necessary." Her thoughts winged back over the years to that day when mutiny broke out, when her cool courage had saved her own life and that of Jenny.

Ayah, ever practical, was already placing chapatties and a drink before her. "Eat, my brave one. You have already ridden far, and without strength you can do nothing."

Andhra forced down a few mouthfuls of the flat bread cake, drank deeply, kissed her little son and said, "If neither Ranjana nor I returns, make all speed with him to my father's palace in the north. He will welcome you both." Then, without wasting more time, she hurried down and out, watered the horse and set off again on her dangerous mission.

It was now the hottest part of the day. In addition, the track wound uphill. Perspiration poured from both her and the horse as they made their way through the ruined plantation and reached the silent thatched huts of the workers.

Not a man, woman or child was left now. Not a chicken was scratching or a piglet rooting. Despair almost overwhelmed her as the realization of Ranjana's bright hopes all dashed swept over her.

But there was no time to think of that now. All her resolution was needed for what lay ahead. After the huts and a strip of land given over to coolie plots, now mere brown deserts, came the river, dividing the palace land from the strip of jungle where Ranjana had once lain in wait for the man-eater. The river was a dry stony bed, easy to cross now. Even the deep water hole where the animals came to drink at dusk was a mere puddle.

Once across the dividing line, the deep hush of the jungle closed in on her. She pressed on along the slight trail made by the Kerbuls, without any real fear of meeting a tiger or any such dangerous creature. They would all be resting in their lairs deep in the shade until the cool of evening drew them forth to seek and stalk their prey.

It would have been pleasant in this green twilight, shut in by tall trees and luxuriant creepers, but for the stifling heat and the insects disturbed by the horse's footsteps that rose up to plague her, but she scarcely noticed them. Her thoughts lay ahead. What would her reception be?

She emerged from the jungle to a high, stony outcrop that doubtless concealed the lair of the Kerbuls. With great caution she followed the still-rising track until she found herself on the highest point, where she drew rein and stood surveying the scene.

Below her was a hollow of land, dotted with trees and crossed by a stream, now almost dry. A ring of thorn bush enclosed a number of dilapidated huts, the larger one in the center no doubt belonging to the chief.

Carefully she dismounted, looped the reins over the branch of a dead tree and began to descend. In which hut were the two men incarcerated, she wondered.

The encampment was as quiet as the jungle. Doubtless the tribe had feasted too well on the stolen food and were now sleeping it off in the shade of their huts. But it was too much to hope that she could descend to it without detection on the stony track. A falling scrap of rock gave her away, and a mangy cur came leaping from one of the huts to stand snarling with bared fangs a few inches from her.

She was not kept long in fear. A near-naked Kerbul came dashing from the same hut as the dog, to stare in wonder at this unexpected intrusion. He began to laugh and jabber in a strange dialect of the south, which she could not follow, but his meaning, when he grabbed hold of her and began to draw her down to his hut, was all too clear.

"Let me go!" she demanded. "I have a message for your chief."

To her great relief, the chief himself, the man who had taken her jeweled Star of Randevi by force, now came striding up to land a blow on his minion's head that sent him packing. Then he gave a mocking salute to his unexpected visitor.

"So, Princess! Have you come to join your husband, or to beg a meal because we took your food?" he asked in a language she could just follow.

"Neither. I have an order for his release from his uncle, the nawab of Cochpur, duly signed and sealed. Unless you hand him over immediately, also Pearson sahib, an armed sortie will be sent to wipe you out."

She fished out the order and handed it over. He read it with some difficulty but was clearly impressed by the signature and the seal. He had seen both before and knew that swift retribution followed any disobeying of the powerful ruler's decrees.

"So rumor is not to be trusted," he said at length. "The family feud cannot be serious. I must do as the nawab commands, for he is a cruel man and has many men and guns at his disposal. You may have the two men, but the food we keep, for we are starving."

"Keep the food but give me the jewel you took from me!" she demanded bravely. "You cannot eat gold and jewels."

He laughed harshly, seemed about to refuse, then shrugged, changing his mind. "Verily, I want no trouble from the nawab. Take it, then. You are a brave woman and deserve it. Very few venture into our midst, yet you come alone."

He fished the star from some inner hiding place and handed it to her. Scarcely daring to believe her luck, she quickly secreted it as he turned and bawled an order.

The next moment another of his tribe appeared with Robert and Ranjana in his wake. Their hands were tied behind their backs and their eyes blindfolded.

A great surge of joy welled through Andhra. They were both fit and well, and about to be freed.

The chief cut the rope binding their hands with his scimitar, tore the bandages from their eyes and said sourly, "Get you gone, and never venture into my stronghold again."

Both men blinked, staring in stupefaction at Andhra. "How did you manage it?" the prince asked, his warm brown eyes on her lovely face.

"I'll tell you on the way home. Come, before he changes his mind," she urged.

The chief refused them horses, so Andhra rode slowly while the two men walked downhill at her side. She told them the whole story, leaving them marveling at her courage and the timely help from Rakhee.

"I can't believe the old rascal is dead," Ranjana said. "Now perhaps we'll be left in peace to live our lives."

"What life?" Robert said cynically, pausing and staring about him as they reached the estate and the full scale of the drought disaster registered. "I think we would be well advised to shake the dust of the south from our feet and start afresh in Darjeeling."

"Perhaps you are right," Ranjana agreed somberly. "Andhra

and the baby could go to her father until we find a place fit for them. It will be a struggle, with so much money lost in this venture."

"No!" Andhra burst out. "Are you men or mice! I know how dear to Ranjana's heart this project is. We'll start again and win through somehow."

"With what, my brave princess?"

"With this!" She flashed her jewel in front of them. "It will bring a great many rupees if it is sold in the right market—rupees to buy more seed and saplings, to pay wages and keep the palace going until the estate brings in some return."

He stared in astonishment. "Truly you are a witch if you coaxed that from the Kerbul chief in his own lair. Your wit is as great as your beauty, my pearl."

"And now, to cap all, I do believe the monsoon is about to break at last!" Robert cut in, his gaze on the inky cloud that was covering the sky above, unnoticed in the press of events.

It was indeed so. Great drops of warm rain began to fall on their upturned faces, rapidly forming a solid sheet of water that covered the parched earth and bounced up again in foot-high drops.

They made no move to escape its fury. So welcome was the deluge that they stood soaked to the skin, reveling in all the good that would come of it. The earth would blossom again. Rivers and rice paddies would fill to overflowing. The iron-hard ground could be tilled afresh with their water buffaloes, oxen and primitive plows. Rice and other crops could be planted and would flourish. Livestock would be seen again and life return to normal. Above all, tea saplings could be set again in the soft earth.

"So much for your talk of quitting!" Andhra chided the two men. "Now say you'll stay and start again. With Balbir's evil influence gone, we'll engage more coolies and regain their full cooperation. I can visualize all those plans we made coming to fruition in due course, and think what a magnificent estate we can build for Sanjay by the time he is old enough to take over."

Ranjana scarcely heard. He was already deep in plans for the future as he and Robert strode on through the rain toward the palace.

But Andhra, seated on her horse, remained as still as a statue for a moment, hands clasped before her face, giving thanks to all the many gods of heaven and earth for bringing them through so many vicissitudes to safety at last.